GRAVEYARD SHIFT

HOPE SZE MEDICAL CRIME NOVEL 7

MELISSA YI

Windtree
Press

Join Melissa's mailing list at www.melissayuaninnes.com

Copyright © 2019 by Melissa Yuan-Innes

Published by Olo Books in association with Windtree Press

Cover photo by boscorelli © 2014 | Deposit Photos

Cover design © 2019 by Design for Writers

Yi, Melissa, author   Graveyard Shift / Melissa Yi.
(Hope Sze crime novel; 7)
Issued in print and electronic formats.
ISBN 978-1-927341-76-6, (softcover).—ISBN 978-1-927341-77-3 (PDF)
    I. Title.   C813'.6

To advise of typographical errors, please contact olobooks@gmail.com

For Elana Fric

Hospitals are only an intermediate stage of civilization, never intended at all even to take in the whole sick population.

— Florence Nightingale

A hospital alone shows what war is.

— Erich Maria Remarque

1

"I just need a refill, doc." The emaciated, over-tanned woman glared at me from the black vinyl bed of St. Joseph's ER exam room number 4. "I ran out over the holidays. My stomach hurts so bad, I want to puke."

"Right, Ms. Goody," I said, eyeing the crumpled bag of chips she'd tossed at the garbage can and missed. Whenever the triage nurse wants to indicate that the patient's 10/10 abdominal pain is B.S., she'll write, *Says pain 10/10. Eating chips.*

And guess what? Narcotic addicts often complain about stomach pain, nausea, and vomiting.

It was 23:06, Lori Goody was my inaugural patient on my first emergency room night shift back in Montreal, and I was in no mood for bull when I had nine horrid hours to go.

I handed back her empty, yellow pill bottle. "The problem is, you refilled this prescription a week ago. You should have enough Dilaudid to last you until next month. It's only January eleventh."

The patient pushed herself into a sitting position, her brown eyes narrowed behind fake eyelashes. Since she looked like Miss Anorexia, I secretly marvelled that she had enough muscle mass to prop herself up. "What's your problem? You a doctor?"

"Yes. I'm Dr. Sze." I showed her my badge and adjusted the stethoscope hung around the back of my neck. "We're trying not to prescribe narcotics because over 17,000 Americans died from prescription opioids in 2017." It hit Canada, too—about half that number in the past two years—although most of them overdosed on synthetic Fentanyl bought unlabeled on the street. "Ms. Goody, I checked the blood work from your last visit. Your potassium was slightly high—"

She waved her hand at me. "I heard of you. Hope Sze." She pronounced it like Zee, which is close enough. "You're the one who's always running around with murderers."

Stung, I said, "I don't *run around*. I've solved a few cases—"

"Get me a real doctor. One who's not in school anymore, and one who doesn't think she's the police."

I glanced at the door behind me. I could grab the supervising physician. Even though I'm a doctor, I'm what used to be called an intern, and I think patients have the right to refuse trainees.

On the other hand, I'd have to bug Dr. Chia, who was finishing up her evening shift with me on the ambulatory, or walk-in, side. I'd already messed up an intubation with Dr. Chia at the beginning of my medical residency six months ago.

No, I'd battle it out for a few minutes with a narcotic-seeking patient instead of immediately weeping on my staff. I tried to smile. "Ms. Goody, I am an M.D. doing my post-graduate residency training—"

"Right. You're a resident. That's useless. Get me the real doctor."

I sucked in my cheeks and checked the door to my left and then the one behind me again, wishing that Lori Goody would take off.

The white-walled examining room barely felt big enough for the two of us plus the examining room bed, a chair, and the newly-added ledge that squashed me against the right wall as I checked the monitor for St. Joe's brand new electronic record system, SARKET.

"Got it? Or maybe you no understand Engleesh?" The patient jabbed a pink acrylic nail at me.

Oh, my God. She'd noticed my Asian heritage and was trying to mimic a Chinese accent. My instinct was to face punch her, but as a doctor, you have to act professionally and smile even though patients will report you at the drop of a nun's cap.

"Maybe because you're too busy making *Fentanyl?*"

Ugh. She must have read those headlines like *China Is Poisoning America With Fentanyl.* I gazed at her, ignoring her T-shirt slogan, BL♣W ME, I'M IRISH. "Actually, China made Fentanyl a controlled substance, Ms. Goody—"

"For fuck's sake. Get me the real doctor. My heart is racing. You're giving me a heart attack." She placed her palm on her chest and hyperventilated, exaggerating the stringy tendons of her neck as well as minimal boobage.

Lori Goody was 35 years old. She'd only have a heart attack with seriously nasty genes and/or cocaine and speed.

Although, speaking of drugs, she had that look, the one my new boyfriend, Tucker, called "rode hard and put away wet": bleached brown hair, darker skin than me even though she was white enough to insult my ancestry, uneven teeth, frosted pink lipstick that might have looked good a few decades ago, and grimy running shoes with no socks despite the icy January weather.

I approached her cautiously, reaching for the navy stethoscope draping the back of my neck. "I can listen to your heart—"

She seized both ends of the stethoscope and wrenched them in opposite directions, to strangle me.

2

I immediately brought my fists together between us and tried to knock her arms away. Kind of like Wonder Woman banging her magic bracelets together and then spreading her arms apart.

I'd taken a few self-defence classes, but learned this move while practicing Akido with my friend Ginger. Also, external shoulder rotators are stronger than internal rotators. I knew that from our clinical methods course, when I practiced on another small, female medical student.

The problem was, Lori Goody had crossed both ends of the stethoscope so tightly around my neck, I couldn't wedge my fingers between the rubber tube and my own skin. The only way I could get any leeway was to press on my own throat, indenting it to try and wiggle under the stethoscope.

Not going to happen.

C'mon, Hope. Time to change tactics.

I dug my nails into her fingers to pry them off. I had long, strong nails, and I was willing to draw blood.

She didn't seem to feel my attempts to carve up her digits. Her grip tightened.

This close, her eyes glittered with glee, even more manic behind those half-inch eyelashes. She cackled. "I'm going to kill you! I'm going to dance in your blood!"

You'll never get a prescription that way, I thought, but as I gasped, she wound it tighter.

My brain grew hazy. My vision darkened at the edges.

I'd faced down killers before, and I was going to die like this? Strangled by an opioid addict with my own stethoscope?

Hell, no.

I grabbed her shoulders and kneed her in the stomach with everything I had. Her wiry abdominal muscles caved in.

She bent over with a silent gasp. The pressure eased a little, but not enough.

I drove my right thumb into her closest eye. It gave a pulpy squish.

She screeched so loudly that it made my eardrums crinkle up in horror, but the important part was that her hands loosened, and I could breathe again.

I stumbled backwards, spots in my vision. My stethoscope fell to the floor, its diaphragm banging on my toes, but I didn't care. As long as that weapon was away from my throat, I could afford to replace a stethoscope. *Add it to my line of credit, sir.*

I backed up so I could keep an eye on Lori Goody while I wrenched the door handle with my right hand. Now I thanked God for a tiny room. It made the exits literally two footsteps away.

"Oh, no you don't." Lori Goody leapt toward me, displaying her crooked teeth and—where did she get that?—a green-handled disposable scalpel, its steel blade pointed directly at me. "I'm going to cut your tits off."

What a bizarre thing to say. I flung the door open. Since it hinged inward, I had to take a step back to escape into the hall.

Dr. Callendar, a dreadful family medicine doctor who moonlit in the emergency room, stood framed in the doorway, blocking my exit. "What is going on—"

He broke off as Lori Goody lunged toward me.

I shoved Dr. Callendar backward as I scrambled for freedom. If he wanted to chat, or do hand to hand combat, better him than me.

Dr. Callendar was bigger than me, at least 5'7", but he put up no resistance, so we ended up stumbling into the hallway in a sort of human snowball, him, me, and a screeching Lori Goody, who yanked my hair backwards so hard that my scalp screamed and my neck spasmed as she jerked me upright.

I blocked out the agony. I reached for the claws of the beast ironically named Lori Goody, trying to imprison them.

I twisted my body clockwise as best I could with my hair still clenched.

I had to know where the scalpel was.

I caught a glimpse of the green scalpel handle. She was right-handed. That arm was coming down.

I brought my left arm up in a hard block, into her inner wrist. *Thank you, Ginger.*

"Bitch!" Lori Goody squeezed out, but her wrist flexed and her fingers spasmed open. The scalpel hit the floor.

She lunged for it, then changed her mind and charged me, snarling, with both hands raised in the air.

I kicked her still-tender stomach. Actually, she came at me so fast, I ended up kneeing her and belatedly extending my leg as she keeled over.

"Dr. Sze!" Dr. Callendar shouted.

Typical that he'd scream at me while a patient literally tried to stab me in the back and/or carve off my breasts.

"Code White," I thundered back at him as loudly as possible with a mashed throat. That was Callendar's cue to alert everyone that a patient was out of control. A Code White immediately summoned security, not to mention orderlies, nurses, and a doctor to pin this nutbar down (physical restraints) and start drugging the bejeezus out of her (chemical restraints).

Hell, with someone this insane, we needed the police. Preferably all of them.

Dr. Callendar stayed sprawled on the floor outside ambulatory room number 4, still hollering at me, but a nurse took up the call.

"CODE WHITE. CODE WHITE. AMBULATORY SIDE," she

shouted, and the nurses on both halves of the ER stared at us for a microsecond before one of them broke toward us, and the rest began to swarm.

Meanwhile, Lori Goody bent over her sore stomach, covering one eye, panting beside Dr. Callendar, but her good eye lasered in on me. "I'm gonna kill you." She started to run, so I ran, too, toward the opposite side of the ER.

There was a wide double door between the ambulatory (walk-in) and acute (ambulance) sides of the ER. That was how we wheeled patients out for X-rays or up to the floor. I could have swerved right beside the old X-ray light boxes and punched open that door, fleeing the emerg altogether. Only another short right would take me down the hall and straight out the ER exit, streaking past a startled security guard.

But what if Lori Goody chased me outside, into the night?

What if the security guard had left his post to scratch his balls?

I couldn't count on waiting patients to do anything except sit and stare as she eviscerated me with a scalpel.

Behind me, she swore, "I'm gonna fuckin' kill you. I'll cut your eyes out, I'll eat your nipples—"

I flinched, but I wouldn't freeze like Dr. Callendar.

I dashed for the nursing station on the acute side, a loose circle of counter space topped by Plexiglass, while the clerk with the punk rock haircut gaped at me, and more nurses and orderlies converged on Lori Goody.

"Code White! Code White!" I yelled at their backs, like a raspy jockey urging them to gallop toward the finish line.

Soon a blessedly flat woman's voice sounded over the loudspeakers. "Code White, Emergency Department. *Code Blanc, Salle D'urgence.*"

"It's okay, Hope, it's okay," said Julie, a female préposée, or orderly, as she shouldered past me, which almost made me laugh.

Anyone with eyes (and Lori Goody might only half fall into this category now) could tell that it wasn't rainbows and moonbeams outside exam room 4.

I had to escape from Lori Goody without putting everyone else in jeopardy.

"Call the police!" I snapped at Julie.

I needed a weapon.

I cast my eyes around the acute side, the side where the bedridden patients lay in stretchers around the perimeter of the room, plus anywhere else we could fit them around the nursing station.

I ignored the paperwork and clipboards strewn over the countertops—useless, unless I thought I could briefly blind her with a blizzard of faxes and reports.

I bypassed the three new computers for SARKET. Also worthless, unless I wanted to heave an LED screen at her.

I did once hear of a PCP patient who ripped out an old school TV embedded in the wall. Another PCP-er strapped to the bed in five-point restraints somehow managed to flip himself into standing position with the bed on his back, like the world's most menacing turtle.

PCP made you that strong and that crazy. Maybe I'd stumbled on Lori Goody's diagnosis. She'd run out of Dilaudid and switched to phencyclidine. PCP was before my time, but maybe drugs were like fashion and cycled in and out every few decades.

My kingdom for a metal urinal. Now, that would have made a decent shield. It was a shame both for safety and the environment that we'd moved on to disposable urinals and bed pans made out of cardboard.

Finally, I spotted someone's iPad on the counter, open to MDCalc. The owner would kill me, but at this point, I'd take a delayed death over one in the next five minutes. I seized the iPad as my shield. It had a case and a glass front. That would do.

I whipped around to check where Lori Goody had gone. Ouch. Pain pierced my neck, but I ignored it, scanning the room.

Dr. Callendar was so useless, he might have continued her history and physical exam and gotten stabbed in the *cojones* for his troubles.

Ah. If only one good thing would come out of tonight.

Kidding. But I permitted myself a small smile. It felt like Tucker and I were under constant attack. Why not let the bad guys take a hit once in a while?

Back on the ambulatory side, maybe fifty feet away—I wasn't good with distances—I peered at the scrum of white coats, green scrubs, hair, and twisting arms and legs, at the ambulatory side's mini nursing station, which was really a countertop with rolling stools. They'd turned it into an L shape with an extra computer because of SARKET, but that counter "arm" blocked my view and trapped them in a smaller area.

"Get her arm!" shouted Dr. Chia.

Lori Goody had twisted Dr. Chia's lab coat and, even from halfway across the bay, it looked like LG might break the doctor's wrist.

"I've got her arm. *Aughh!*" That was Dr. Callendar again. He'd started climbing to his feet before LG caught him under the chin. He tipped backward, his black hair headed straight for the ground again.

"Where are all the guards?" a nurse screamed. "Aren't we supposed to have a thousand of them after the OR?"

What happened in the operating room?

Meanwhile, Dr. Chia, Dr. Callendar, two nurses, and the small orderly all tried to pin Lori Goody to the floor. The problem was, with so little room, they bashed into rolling stools and even into each other while she bit and kicked and punched and spat, scaring them into loosening their grip.

I approached cautiously, holding the iPad in front of my chest.

As soon as Lori Goody caught sight of me, she gave a tonsil-rattling howl and struggled upright before the orderly, who was barely taller than my five foot two, somehow knocked her feet out from under her.

LG landed, keening, on her ass.

"Get out of here, Hope," called Dr. Chia.

"I can medicate her. Haldol and Ativan." What the hell. She'd been asking for drugs. We could give them to her, only not the refill she wanted.

"A nurse is on it. You get out. You're making her crazy."

She was already there. Still, I reluctantly backed away, iPad blocking my chest (and nipples) as the security guards rushed in. There's a security guard posted right by the ER entrance, maybe another 30 feet away if you cut through the small triage room, so you'd expect them to arrive immediately, but most of them look 200 years old. Speed is not their forte.

We got younger ones this time, a grey-haired, sixtyish white man and a tall, young white guy with glasses and an Adam's apple that seemed to jut from his throat.

"Slow and easy does it," the older guy was saying. He had a pair of handcuffs in his right hand, already open for business. "They've got her. We cuff her wrists, and then we can get her feet."

He was talking instead of moving.

Go for it, I silently urged him.

Instead, he gestured at the young guard to open his own set of cuffs. The young guy's hands trembled, and he said, "I don't want an incident."

Dear God. This was not a teachable moment.

"It's not an *incident,* Patrick. It's our job," said the old guard.

I backed further out of range and muttered, "Make them tight." Lori Goody was so skinny, I bet they could use child-sized cuffs on her.

The young security guard opened the cuffs, but he didn't place them over her wrists, even though she pummelled the air and nearly made contact with the orderly's shoulder.

The old guard gestured for Patrick to hurry up, waving his own handcuffs in the air instead of using them.

"Come on," I ground out between my teeth. If it took any longer, I'd have to knock her out with the iPad.

"I've got her, Patrick!" called Julie, who clamped Lori Goody's wrists, like a champ.

"We got her. Move in," the old guard said, but neither of them had managed to touch the patient. "Don't let New Year's get you down, Patrick. We got this. It's our job."

A new, young nurse yelped.

"She bit Amber," Dr. Chia called. "Amber, you get out and wash the bite. I'll write you some Clavulin afterward."

"I'll do it," I said. I hated hanging back helplessly. Writing a prescription was lame, but better than standing at the sidelines and calling, Olé, olé!

The mound of people on the floor started writhing in earnest as Lori Goody ululated once more, and Dr. Chia said, "Hope, *you* don't do anything except *get out of here.*"

I stood rooted. If this were my fault, I'd do what I could to get them out of it.

"Out. Now!" Dr. Chia roared, and I beat my way back through the growing crowd to the acute side and set the iPad on the counter where I'd found it. At least it had met a gentler fate than Amber, who blinked back tears as one of my favourite nurses, Roxanne, cleaned the bite with Chlorhexidine.

"Make sure you wash it with tons of soap and water," I told them. As we used to say in medical school, the solution to pollution is dilution. Amber needed fewer fancy cleansing products and more old-fashioned scrubbing. Human bites were dirty, and who knew what (or whom) Lori Goody had last eaten.

Roxanne, a petite, fine-boned RN who often joked about her Italian grandmother, had lost her usual grin. She gave me a quick nod, making her wavy brown bob bounce.

Take home lesson: do not mess with nurses. They will stick together and mess you up.

Take home lesson number two: if you're a doctor, even if someone tries to strangle you, keep on truckin'. No one will kiss it better.

Sad. I shook off the melancholy. My phone buzzed in the pocket over my right bum cheek. I'd missed a few texts during the madness, and now someone was calling me.

I reached for my phone, but someone grabbed my elbow.

I jerked back, ready to wallop him.

A surprised Tucker stared down at me. "You okay, Hope? You weren't answering my texts, so I—what happened to your neck?"

3

I gasped.

My hands jerked toward my neck.

Now that Tucker had mentioned it, and my adrenaline was dying down, just plain breathing scoured my throat. My scalene muscles had seized up. I could hardly speak.

And forget how I must look. I probably sported wild horse eyes and a red-purple necklace of bruises as wide as my stethoscope.

Talking would hurt more, so I did a pantomime for him, pretending to tighten a cord around my own neck.

"You tried to...hang yourself?" he said, eyes widening.

That almost made me laugh. Tucker called us soul mates, and I'd agree 80 percent, but sometimes he got things hilariously wrong. I shook my head and, to save my voice, opened up the Notes app and wrote it down for him on my phone: *Patient tried to strangle me.*

"Are you serious? I mean, of course you're serious, but—"

I rolled my eyes to convey my thoughts, namely, *Why would I joke about this?*

Tucker's fists tightened. "Where is he? Please tell me he's out of here so I don't have to kill him."

I shook my head and pointed at the tangle of people, led by the security guards. It looked like Patrick had finally, finally managed to handcuff her, and now they were working on her ankles.

"That's—it looks like a woman."

I nodded.

"And are the police even here? Is she sedated?"

I shook my head no and no.

"And you're going to do this night shift, even though someone tried to kill you? Again?"

I held my hands palms up at shoulder level in a joint move that meant both "Back off" and possibly "I surrender." If the night doc excused me, I'd probably leave. But if the doc wanted all hands on deck, I'd stay. That was my job. Although how much good I'd do working mute, I couldn't say.

My phone buzzed and buzzed in my hand. Someone really wanted to talk to me. I almost never answered my cell in the emergency room, but what if something had happened to my parents or my little brother, Kevin?

"You're going down, bitch!" Lori Goody hollered as they rolled her past me, strapped onto a stretcher, into our psychiatry room. Unfortunately, that placed her in the acute side's room 14, almost directly across from me and Tucker. "You think you can get away with it?"

Get away with what? A night shift?

"I'm gonna tell Guillaume about you! He'll squish you like a—like a Chinese cockroach!"

Ugh. I doubted she'd wrestle her racist butt out of her five point restraints and make a phone call. Why hadn't they placed a face mask over her nose and mouth? It wasn't for every Code White, but when they started trying to stab you, surely we had to break out every defence available. Not only would a mask prevent her from spitting on them and discourage biting, but it might muffle some of her braying, too.

I was more worried about my persistent phone caller. The 613 area code number looked familiar enough that I answered the next call, even though it wasn't my parents, and I was trying to save my vocal cords.

A woman said, her voice taut with fear, "Hope. Is Ryan with you?"

My hand tightened on the phone. Tucker's my man now, but I'll love Ryan Wu forever, even after I'm dead and I'm nothing but sun-bleached bones. I forced my vocal cords to adduct. "Hi, Mrs. Wu. No, I'm working. He's not here."

"He's not—but where—Rick, he's not there!" She hung up.

I stared at my phone's flat, black screen in shock. I'd never heard Ryan's mother so panicked. She was a peaceful piano and voice teacher who volunteered at church and made better dumplings than my own grandmother. Ten days after Ryan and I broke up, I ran into her in the grocery store. She hugged me and said into my hair, "I'll always want the best for you, Hope," while her husband nodded awkwardly and stood three feet away.

She shouldn't have spoken to me at all. Ryan had cut me off. He'd blocked my number and my barely-used social media accounts. His friends Terry and Malcolm had immediately unfriended me on Facebook, and I'm sure everyone else did, too. So Cheryl Wu wouldn't call me in the middle of the night unless it was urgent.

And she had told me why.

Ryan was missing. The other half of my heart had vanished.

I knew that anyone who jumped in here on a TV series of my life would wonder what in the blue blazes was going on and why I couldn't pick one team, Tucker or Ryan.

It's complicated. I love both Ryan Wu and John Tucker more than my own soul. Ryan was my first boyfriend, and I will go to my grave loving him. But Tucker and I have been through absolute hell together, including 14/11, a hostage taking on November 14th so excruciating that I can only refer to it by a number. Even flying home from Los Angeles nearly killed us—and Tucker and I ended up sort of engaged.

Which means I'm monogamous with Tucker now. I know it doesn't compute, but neither does anything else I touch.

In response, Ryan slashed me out of his life. Totally understandable.

He's the perfect man. Well, perfect except that I'm agnostic and he used to be the World's #1 Christian. That meant he wanted to marry me and have two to four kids. He already had a loving foster dog, Roxy. So he was mega-trustworthy and he was so hot that it hurt to look at him. It doesn't get any better than that.

I still ached for Ryan every day, every minute. Tucker took me out for Indian food one night, and all I could do was cry because the pakoras reminded me of Ryan.

I'd assumed Ryan would be okay. Destroyed like I was, yes. But fuelled by righteous fury and surrounded by dozens of pure and lovely church girls, he'd mend faster than I would.

Instead, he'd now disappeared so thoroughly that he'd panicked his own parents.

I called Mrs. Wu back, ignoring the nurse printing an electrocardiogram on one side of us, the clerk paging ICU on the other, Lori Goody threatening to report us all to the College, and Tucker's eyes drilling a hole into my profile.

My call went to voice mail. "Mrs. Wu. You know I haven't heard from Ryan in two weeks—" And three days and twelve hours. My throat spasmed. I missed him so much that I could hardly speak, even before Lori Goody tried to take me down. "He, uh, blocked my number." He wouldn't even pick up when I called from my friend Tori's phone, or a pay phone. He probably refused to respond to all numbers from Montreal's area code, 514. "But if he shows up, I'll call you right away. Let me know how long he's been missing, and if you have any leads, and..."

Most people wouldn't rocket into 911 mode when their ex-boyfriends melted away. But if you were Dr. Hope Sze and had barely survived a gun to your temple, you'd go nuclear.

"...tell him I love him."

My voice broke again. Why did I say that?

Because it was true.

I could delete that message, but fuck it. It was true. If nothing else, I told the truth.

I hung up instead, my heart banging like a rabbit trying to kick its way out of my chest.

I couldn't look at Tucker.

He swore until he ran out of breath.

What could I say? *I love you, too. Insanely, insatiably, but not exclusively.* All of it was true, but it wouldn't help.

Tucker threw back his stool and started pacing. I wouldn't blame him if he ditched me, too.

I felt like a toxic waste dump.

I poisoned everything and everyone I loved. Tucker would be better off without me.

Bebe Rexha's "I'm a Mess" rang in my ears. I had it on my phone on replay during my crying jags.

Unfortunately, I needed to get back to work.

"I love you. I'm sorry," I whispered, and turned to the rack of charts. At night, they consolidated the patients' charts, both ambulatory and acute, on the acute side.

Tucker watched me, simmering with rage.

I said over my shoulder, "I'm sorry. I love you."

The rack of clipboards blurred before my eyes. Because St. Joe's SARKET computerized record system was so new, they had a hybrid system where they printed out a sheet with each patient's ID, health card number, and chief complaint, but you had to type up the complete history and physical and enter orders on either a desktop computer or a WOW ("workstation on wheels"). It was originally called a COW, or computer on wheels, until they decided that was insulting to our bovine friends.

I made my way toward the ambulatory exam rooms. They were so small that you couldn't wheel in a WOW. You had to use the computer within the room or write or dictate later at the desktops. The nursing station counter was so miniature, only two people could fit comfortably on the main part of the L.

If Dr. Chia returned to work on these desktops, Tucker would have to move, or slide over to a third stool. And if the big male nurse, Bill, happened to work ambulatory, the rest of us would end up crammed on the other end. Maybe that was why he never came over here.

I stared at my next chart, a 24-year-old male with a sore throat. My eyes blurred. *Dude, I know all about sore throats.*

I tapped on the escape key, waking up the desktop computer to register myself as the MD looking after this patient. Because of the computerized system, I now had to wait until Amber was triaged and registered as a patient before I could prescribe her Clavulin.

When I walked to exam room 1 for the sore throat, Tucker reappeared by my side.

"Hope," he said.

I turned to him, blushing already.

"It's not okay," he said, struggling to control his face and his voice. His brown eyes burned with hostility. "But I know something's up. What happened to Ryan?"

I closed my eyes, trying not to let the tears out. *Tucker still loves me.*

He immediately reached for my hair, sweeping my bangs off my forehead. We didn't even brush hands at work, because all he had to do was look at me, and Roxanne would hoot, "Get a room!" But we both craved that brief touch.

"I don't know," I whispered. My throat felt like Lori Goody had taken a cheese grater to it.

"Hope, we said no more secrets."

I exhaled. Transparency. That's what Tucker had said, actually. *One hundred percent transparency.* And I'd told him that was unrealistic. Everyone needed some privacy, a bit of mystery, for heaven's sake.

He'd gazed at me with those brown eyes—such a marked contrast from his wheat blond hair—and he'd said, "I don't."

Maybe that was true because he truly wanted to mind-meld with me. Maybe it wasn't. Either way, tonight I was stuck in the emergency department until at least 8 a.m. If I told Tucker what was going down, maybe he could start searching for Ryan.

Which Ryan would hate. He was proud. He was the opposite of Tucker, more like a panther.

Quiet. Private. Stalking his prey. A beast in bed.

Tucker was a party in your face. *Woo hoo! I brought the beer! Not*

Molson's, but a microbrew called Minot, made in tiny batches in my new friend's basement! Best beer of your life!

I said, "Ryan's missing."

Tucker's body turned rigid.

"His mom called me. Shows you how desperate they are." I leaned into him and pressed my eyes into his scrub top, letting the tears soak in, even though I'd probably get conjunctivitis from his work clothes. I felt like I deserved it.

He wrapped his arms around my shoulders, kissing my forehead. Although he'd been working for the past 16 hours, he still smelled like soap and deodorant, along with the faint note of his sweat. I inhaled his scent, which gave me the courage to say, "I'm working. Could you—"

Tucker exhaled. He and Ryan had been fighting over me since, mmm, August. So less than six months. Not that long, but very, very intense.

"Unless you want my emerg shift?" I joked into his chest. Both of us had missed too much work since we were taken hostage November 14th. The faculty was working with us to make sure we graduated on time, but Tucker was out of action for two months after two surgeries. He wrote a paper and made one month a research block, but neither of us could miss any more clinical time without Serious Consequences.

Tucker didn't reply for an agonizingly long moment, making me hold my breath.

At last, when he exhaled again, his core muscles contracted so much that his abdomen no longer made contact with mine. He was withdrawing from me.

My eyes spewed some more tears, but I didn't dare wipe them on him. I pulled away and let them fall down my face.

Tucker's rough voice cut through the air, stopping me. "Do you have any more details about him? When was the last time they had contact with him, what was he doing, did he leave a note—"

"Nothing," I whispered, and I was crying in earnest. Ryan had sliced me out of his life. It was like an exorcism.

Tucker placed his fingers on my back with excessive care. He loathed my longing for Ryan, but he knew he couldn't excise it. At long last, he said, "Don't worry."

I leaned back to stare into his eyes and examine the lines of his face.

His brow furrowed, his eyes staring into mine. "I'll take care of it."

Ryan was a him, not an it. I opened my mouth.

"He's not allowed to become a martyr." Tucker stepped away from me.

"Thank you," said the clerk, who made a show of squeezing around us to scoop up a paper on the counter behind us.

We walked away from the desk, not speaking, but he'd picked up on my fears exactly. What if Ryan was so destroyed by me/us that he'd killed himself?

Not that I considered myself so crucial, but Tucker and I weren't the only ones damaged by 14/11. Ryan lost his faith. In a way, it worked for me, because it meant he gave up abstinence and fell into bed (and into the car, and into the shower) with me.

But now that I'd chosen Tucker again, it had left Ryan with nothing. No woman, and no faith to hold him back from the abyss.

I knew I had to get back to that sore throat patient. I knew that tonight's evaluation was already in the toilet, and that I could fail my year or even my entire residency.

But Ryan was more important. He was one of the human beings I loved the most in the world, even if I could never have him again.

If I had to, I would leave medicine to search for him right here and right now.

So Tucker stepped into the breach. After working for 16 hours, he'd jump into a car to track down his rival in another city, with almost no clue where he was going.

For me. Because he knew that was what I wanted. More than escaping this night shift. More than saving my own skin. I needed Ryan.

I turned to Tucker. "You'll find Ryan."

He gave a curt nod.

"Alive. And sane."

His lips twisted. After a pause, he said, "Well. He's in love with you, isn't he?"

I punched his shoulder. It bounced off in a comical, girly way. For once, I didn't care.

He kissed me and left without saying another word.

4

_____

I could breathe again now that Tucker was searching for my private Ryan.

I raised my hand to rap on the door of exam room 1, but a fiftyish, pretty, pony-tailed brunette nurse named Kris took one look at the chart in my hand and said, "Sore throat? Forget that. You should see the one in 13 first. She's the sickest—at least before the paramedics run out of Narcan, and all the overdoses flood the gates."

How could they run out of the antidote to narcotic overdoses? They sold Narcan, or Naloxone, at pharmacies. The police stocked up on it. A McGill student made headlines by giving free public workshops on how to deliver it up the nose.

Still, I didn't have the vocal cords to quiz Kris about anything but the sick patient.

"What happened to her?" I whispered, obediently taking the chart from her hand.

Kris shoved the sore throat clipboard back in the pile. "Someone beat her up. She won't admit it, though. Says she fell down the stairs." She grimaced. "Won't see ASAP, either."

That was our sexual assault team. We were talking big time. "I'll see what I can do," I murmured, but she probably couldn't hear me over her own sneakers as she hurried to bed 1.

On the acute side, where the ambulances came to play, and where we parked people who couldn't walk anymore, the patients were laid in a clock-like pattern. Beside the barely-used eye room sat our double resuscitation room with two stretchers labelled A and B, also usually deserted, at roughly 10 o'clock.

Then, around the perimeter of our ambulance bay, starting at 11 o'clock, stretchers with curtains were numbered 1 to 11. Three rooms, 12 to 14, extended to 7 o'clock, before the double doors with the light boxes that divided us from the ambulatory side. The sickest patients were usually in beds 1 to 6, on cardiac monitors. I could still hear Lori Goody yowling from 14, our psych room.

If this patient lay in one of our few precious rooms, it meant we were giving her more privacy than the patients jammed in the hallway or in any spare spot around the ambulance bay.

Like anything in the ER, it was a mixed blessing: she got the private room and a doctor's immediate attention because she was in such rough shape.

Good news for me. In a room, I could whisper my way through the history and physical exam. I wouldn't have to compete as much with the beeping monitors, IV's, alarms, or the chat and laughter from the nursing station in the centre of the ambulance side.

That was the idea, anyway.

"You can't beat me up like an *Indian,*" LG called. Then she spotted me heading into the neighbouring room and screamed, "THAT'S HER! Get her!"

I closed the curtain. It didn't muffle LG's commandments, but it made me feel better as I faced my next patient, 24-year-old Alyssa Taylor.

Raccoon eyes.

I sucked in my breath. I'd never seen them in real life before, but her medium brown skin tone couldn't hide the purple, protruding bruising around her eyes.

Medical school had taught me to check for a basilar skull fracture —a break in the bottom of the skull—when I saw raccoon eyes.

Yeah, this was more important than a sore throat. I sent a silent thank you to Kris.

"She's *right here.* Go grab her. This is your chance to *shank* her!"

Alyssa Taylor started, even though I bet Lori Goody was ranting about me.

Still, it meant that Alyssa Taylor was awake and aware, even if she had a break in her skull.

"Don't worry, bae. I won't let her touch you. I won't let anyone touch you," said the tall, thin, white, bespectacled guy I belatedly noticed beside her. He wore a blue shirt, navy pants, and various badges, but the handcuffs and baton at his waist, and especially his Adam's apple bobbing up and down, shocked me into recognition.

He was the younger security guard who'd helped subdue Lori Goody. His badge said PATRICK WARREN.

His girlfriend got beat up? When?

I started to touch her shoulder. She winced, so I stopped mid-air. Tucker once patted a trauma patient's arm and then realized that it was broken. "Sorry. Hi. I'm Dr. Hope Sze. Do you want to talk to me alone first?"

She started to shake her head.

"Don't move your head, please. Just use your voice," I said.

She wore a C-spine collar in case any of her neck bones had fractured along with her skull. The collar did allow some range of motion, though, which is why we always shouted at patients to stay still.

"When did this happen?" I asked, deliberately avoiding Patrick Warren's eyes. If Alyssa had been attacked in the past few minutes, he had an alibi: Lori Goody, who was currently demanding an optometrist, because I'd turned her into a cyclops.

I did feel bad about that. I'm useless without glasses myself. I made a mental note to order an ophthalmology consult.

Alyssa blinked. She fought to breathe through her nose, which was cocked to her right. Dried blood caked her nostrils.

She had to inhale and exhale through her teeth, which were clamped together. She might be in pain in general, or she could have a jaw fracture.

She pointed at Patrick, the security guard and the bae, who jumped in, "She wasn't answering my texts, so I went to check on her on my break—we have a sublet right next to the hospital—"

"When did you have time to do that?" He'd had his hands full with the human AK-47 named Lori Goody.

He bit his lip. "Well, I started at 1900. I was worried, because usually we check in with each other, and she didn't—anyway. At 2200, I popped over. Just to make sure she was okay." He turned his eyes on me, enormous behind his glasses. "Charles covered for me. He's my boss. We're a two minute walk."

Charles must be the grey-haired guy at the Code White. And a pretty good guy, because judging from the way Patrick twitched, either it wasn't an authorized break, or he was nervous about how long it had taken. "And where did you find her?"

"We're in a basement apartment. The door was hanging a bit open. I started yelling her name. She's really careful about locking the door. I thought something happened to her—"

Alyssa's eyes burned at him. It looked even creepier with the bruising ringing her orbits, like she was an angry purple panda.

He broke off and swept a hand through his hair. "But, uh, she says that she fell down the basement stairs. And she couldn't get to her phone."

Alyssa's body relaxed slightly in the stretcher, under her thin sheet. Yes, that was the story she wanted to tell.

"How many stairs was that?" I asked. Most of the housing around the hospital is, at most, two stories high.

"Like I said, we have a basement apartment," Patrick said uncertainly.

"So one flight of stairs," I said, trying not to sound too cynical. Young people have fast reflexes. Even if they fall down a full flight, at most, they fracture their wrists or ankles.

Older women, like in their 60s, don't put their hands out as fast and break their humeruses (humeri?). And the elderly, maybe 70 plus, break their hips.

I'm no trauma expert, but I'd never seen a 24-year-old smash her face like this.

I itched to search for the Battle sign, which is bruising around the mastoid bone, behind the ear. I'd have to wait until a nurse appeared to stabilize her neck. Then we could remove the cervical spine collar long enough for me to check.

"Are you able to talk?" A normal voice is an excellent sign of a good airway, and if she were coherent, I could do a full neurological exam.

"Yes," she mouthed, but she hitched her shoulders and glanced at Patrick.

He turned red. "She asked me to, uh, give the history." History is the medical term for the patient's verbal account of what happened, and physical means the physical exam. Patrick wasn't used to medical words, but he was trying.

"Does your throat hurt?" I asked Alyssa. Mine sure did. Although I tried to keep it to a whisper, I had to override Lori Goody, who had started singing next door. As far as I could tell, it was a mangled version of "The Final Countdown."

Alyssa's mouth shaped another yes, but there was no power behind it.

Falling down the stairs doesn't damage your vocal cords. Lori Goody had injured mine when she tried to strangle me. That's a direct, compressive force.

You shouldn't hurt your throat falling down the stairs. You'll instinctively tuck your chin and roll. There are so many other things to bang instead: your head, your limbs, your butt.

"Were you drinking or doing drugs?" That, at least, would dull your reflexes to throw your hands out as you fell.

She pressed her lips together. The bottom one had split down the middle. I'd have to check her teeth, too.

"Lyss doesn't do any of that stuff. She doesn't smoke, either," Patrick said immediately.

I watched Lyss's eyes. She didn't blink.

No one wanted to admit to drugs except marijuana, but Alyssa showed no signs of overdose. Her pupils were 3 mm, or normal. She seemed alert and intelligent as she followed the conversation.

She glowered at Patrick. If I read her right, she was clean, or clean enough that she wouldn't contradict anything in front of her boyfriend.

I should interview her alone. But I also needed the complete history, which she was unwilling or unable to give herself. Drug and alcohol use weren't the biggest deal, because we'd screen her urine and blood for those.

I wanted the bigger kahuna, which was what had happened to her tonight.

What were the chances that a doctor who couldn't really talk had to take a history from a patient who couldn't really talk?

On a night shift, maybe as high as 20 percent.

I decided to move on to less threatening questions and circle back to the big kahuna. "Are you hurting anywhere else? Your neck?"

She made a face, so I ventured back into the ER to grab a nurse or three.

As soon as I exited the doorway, Lori Goody screeched, "You guys get off on beating us up. I'm going to sue the fuck out of you!"

I tried not to turn toward her or even break my stride. Lori Goody couldn't squeeze any cash out of me. Student debt R Us.

Kris volunteered to stabilize Alyssa's neck while I gently undid the Velcro of her C-spine collar. Roxanne and Andrea, my other favourite nurse, stood by.

I liked to check the neck while the patient was lying flat on her back. If she had absolutely no pain, numbness, tingling, or weakness, even on neck movement, and she wasn't intoxicated or otherwise mentally incompetent, then she could roll herself on her side when I checked the rest of her spine ("the log roll").

Raising my voice made me cough, but I needed Alyssa to hear me and not Lori Goody. "When I touch you, I want you to say yes, I have pain, or no, I don't have pain. Don't nod or shake your head. Say yes or no. Only use your mouth. Okay?"

She started to nod, caught herself, and mouthed, "Yes."

I found two spots of tenderness, C2 and C3. She'd just bought herself a longer stint in the cervical spine collar and some neck X-rays, if not a CT.

I sucked in my breath when I checked her eardrums. The good news was that I couldn't detect any hemotympanum, or blood behind the eardrums, which would have been another sign of a basal skull fracture.

The bad news was that her left ear had been partially ripped off. She cried out when I touched it.

I bit my lip. I've never seen that before. "I'll sew it back on," I promised, but I knew it would be tricky to suture between her ear and her skull. "Let me check for blood clots. You don't want a cauliflower ear."

Boxers used to get those. You had to drain the blood, or the blood clot could cut off the blood supply to the ear cartilage, shrivelling the ear. She did have a centimetre-wide bruise on her left outer ear, but it wasn't a big hematoma, probably because her lacerations had bled it out already.

Then I had to blink back tears when I got to her neck and spotted the tell-tale purple necklace of bruises, with two thumbprints at the base of her throat.

Someone had tried to strangle her.

5

"Could you leave us for a moment?" I asked Patrick Warren, staring into Alyssa Taylor's eyes. I'd redone the C-spine collar, but we all knew what I'd seen and what it meant.

"Um, she doesn't, uh—"

"Just for a few minutes. While we do the log roll," I said.

It wasn't a question. Three nurses stood with me in silent solidarity.

"Um, I guess, if Lyss doesn't mind—"

"I always take some time alone with each patient," I said. It wasn't quite true, but he didn't need to know that. As a security guard, he wouldn't watch us do patient exams.

"I'll step out, but Dr. Sze?" said Patrick.

I realized that I'd been breathing too loudly through my nose. "Yes?"

"I think that—well, she doesn't want me to say this, but—"

"No," said Alyssa Taylor. It was the first word she'd spoken out loud. She had a high voice, but she spoke like iron.

"Lyss, she should know—"

"NO."

"Okay." He sounded defeated, and his magnified eyes darted from side to side. "Okay. Lyss. Whatever you say. I love you. Call me when you want me back in."

The curtain clicked open and closed behind him, and Lori Goody exploded at his retreating back, "Come on! You want to kick me again? Have at it. More money for me!"

I turned back to Alyssa Taylor. "I'm going to check the rest of your spine now. And a rectal exam, which is a finger in your bum."

Her lips shaped some words. I'm not good at lip reading, so I frowned in puzzlement. She seemed to be saying *I can't...*

"You can't," I repeated out loud.

She sighed in exasperation and held up her phone in her right hand.

"She wants to type to you," said Kris.

Sometimes patients used their cell phones to talk, but usually not in the middle of a log roll. I was tying up three nurses, one to secure the neck and two to roll the body, on a night shift, when we had skeletal staff. Still, this was the first time she was trying to communicate with me.

"Sure, no problem. Do you want to type after we roll you?"

"No." She forced the word out.

"Okay. Tell me what you need." I lowered my voice and coughed. If I whispered, it didn't strain my throat too much.

Lori Goody had no such problem next door. "I'm calling the police. I'm charging you with...hospital brutality!"

Well, that was a step up from cutting off my breasts.

Roxanne helped hold Alyssa's phone where she could see it and type. The screen was cracked. I wondered if that had happened before or after her face.

I murmured, "If there's anything else you want to tell me. For example, if you were sexually assaulted—"

She winced and wrote one word.

NO

Well, thanks be for that. Andrea and I exchanged a look.

I said, "You know, if you ever need to call 911, and your broken screen is glitchy, you can activate it with other keys. On my phone, if I press and hold the power button and a volume button, I'll get emergency services. Even if you can't talk, they'll send someone."

Alyssa tapped on more keys, and Roxanne turned the damaged screen toward me. I squinted to read the letters behind broken glass.

just xray me

"I'll do that too," I said, silently adding, *After your pregnancy test.* "Do you want anything for pain while you're waiting?" We should take her urine test beforehand, so that it didn't pick up iatrogenic (hospital-given) narcotics.

Alyssa blinked in agreement before she moved on to the more crucial bit.

I'm going home

"No. You're probably going to be here all night."

no way

I sighed.

"Look," said Kris, in a no-nonsense mom voice. "You're here for us to help you. Let us help you."

Alyssa pursed her torn lips.

I said, "Alyssa, I have to test you. I have to scan your head and neck, I have to X-ray your body, I have to check your throat, sew up any lacerations, and splint any fractures. If anything is too serious, you're going to a trauma centre, and you probably won't be out for days."

She closed her eyes. The lids fused so tightly, I couldn't be sure, but I thought tears shone behind them.

She was hurt, she was tired, and she was alone.

I said, more gently, "Trust us, okay?"

She tried to shake her head before all four of us roared, "Don't shake your head. Say yes or no!"

Finally, Alyssa let Kris count to three while the two other nurses rolled her.

I ran my fingers down Alyssa's spine. She didn't seem to have any point tenderness on her thoracic, lumbar, or sacral spine, but she had bruises on her back, her legs, and her arms.

"Okay. Now I'm going to do the part that nobody likes. It's a finger in your bum."

"No!"

"It's more uncomfortable than painful. I use lubrication," I said. Roxanne had already torn open a pack of Muco Gel and squeezed it on the disposable square piqué pad covering the mattress. I mouthed my thanks at her as I double-gloved, smeared my index finger in gel, and gently inserted it in her rectum, searching for a tear, blood, or a mass.

She cried out.

"I know," said Kris. "Almost done. Almost there. Hang in there."

"I'm sorry. No blood," I reported to the nurses, and threw away my soiled glove. That was why I wore two for the rectal exams.

Andrea helped pull up Alyssa's pants while I searched for words. My mind was locked on an emergency medicine article my friend Tori had showed me, "Non-fatal strangulation is an important risk factor for homicide of women."

It was a tough read, but it boiled down to this: if someone tries to strangle a woman, but doesn't actually kill her, her risk of death rises six or seven times.

So when the woman comes to the ER looking like Rihanna post-Chris Brown, if she's wearing a purple necklace, it's never only a question of Humpty-Dumptying her together again. We have to intervene now, or she may die before she makes it back to one of our stretchers.

More horrifyingly, near-strangling isn't as much of a death risk factor for African-American women because they're already at much higher risk. They are *four times* more likely to have their partner kill or attempt to kill them, period. Doesn't matter whether the guy tried to strangle them before or not. How would you like to be four times more likely to die, based only on the colour of your skin?

Tori had gone on to research how indigenous women were three times more likely to be attacked, but tonight, the statistics looked grim for the black woman in front of me.

"Alyssa," I said.

She laid on the stretcher with her eyes closed against me.

"I have to ask you this. I ask everyone who comes in hurt, male or female, no matter what age, in honour of a Toronto family doctor who was killed by her husband. Is Patrick hurting you?"

Her eyes shot open. She grabbed her phone, turned it on, and shoved it in my face, pointing at the *NO*.

"Okay. Is someone else hurting you?"

This time, she hesitated before she pointed at the *NO*.

The pause could be a sign, however slight. I gestured at her neck and her ear and her body. "Could you please tell me how this happened?"

She paused again.

Tell me, tell me, tell me throbbed in my brain.

I could feel the nurses' and my collective will pulsing at her. I held my breath.

Her eyes broke away from mine. She thumbed the word at me: *NO*.

I exhaled. Okay. It was hard to trust someone at first glance and confess your deepest secrets, especially when that someone started interrogating you and sticking a finger up your butt.

Maybe she'd tell me later.

More likely, she'd tell one of the nurses.

"If you change your mind, we're here all night," I whispered. "We're good listeners."

She typed another word: *patrick*

Roxanne tiptoed toward the door. "I'll get him."

"Good idea." Even if Alyssa wouldn't tell us anything right now, Patrick might be scared enough to let something slide.

But as I washed my hands at the sink, I surveyed the ambulance bay and couldn't detect any trace of him.

6

"That's strange," said Kris. "You'd think if he was so concerned about her—"

"I know." I frowned. It made me think of my own Gone Boy, though, so after I dried my hands, I took a quick peek at my phone. Nothing from Ryan, and nothing about Ryan from Tucker. I closed my eyes and prayed.

I love you, man. Be safe.

I wasn't even sure which man I was talking about. Either. Both.

Otherwise, I was hating the parallels on this night shift.

Someone had tried to strangle me, and someone had tried to strangle Alyssa Taylor.

My ex-boyfriend was missing, and Alyssa Taylor's current boyfriend was missing.

To be fair, maybe Patrick had gone back to work, and I didn't have time to look for him. Still, I cast an uneasy glance at Room 13 and 14. Roxanne had returned to room 14 to sedate Lori Goody again.

At least I knew exactly who had tried to wring my neck.

The question was who'd gone after Alyssa Taylor. She wouldn't tell us, but her boyfriend might.

If he hadn't disappeared.

Well, I wasn't sure of his hours, but if he started at 1900, he might do a 12 hour shift and finish at 0700. That gave me over six hours to pry the story out of him, because face it, he'd be easier to crack than Alyssa.

She knew who'd beaten her, but for whatever reason, she wouldn't talk.

Patrick knew. And he'd talk. Because he'd want them punished.

"If we don't have an extra security guard right now, could we at least get a sitter for Alyssa?" I asked Kris. I didn't want Alyssa alone, and bruised, and scared. "Even—what about that, uh, male nurse who usually sits here? Bill, right?" I pointed at the chair at the nursing station nearest the resus room. We have an obese, perpetually irritated male nurse who spends most of his shift parked in the chair at the end of the nursing station near resus A and B. He knows what he's doing, but I try to minimize my interaction with him. He seems to hate residents, or at least me. "Is he working today?"

Kris shook her head. "Bill's gone. He's done."

Her tone was a bit odd, but before I could ask, Lori Goody screeched, "I'M GOING TO SUE YOU! I'M GOING TO SUE EVERY LAST MOTHERFUCKING ONE OF YOU!"

"Please do," said Roxanne, as she left room 14, shaking her head.

"You gave her Haldol and Ativan?" I asked.

"Twice," she said, her brown eyebrows drawing together. "She's skinny, but she's like an elephant. We're waiting for her drug screen to come back."

Right. Who knew what she'd mainlined at home while waiting for a refill. "We'll have to step it up with benzos, at least. Let me talk to Dr. Chia, if she's still here."

I made my way to the ambulatory side desk, where Dr. Chia had abandoned her lab coat on her chair. I knew it was hers. Not only did it have her name embroidered above the front pocket and EMERGENCY MEDICINE across the back, which was useful when patients kept asking if you're a nurse, but she'd paid extra to have a red rhythm strip embroidered between her shoulder blades, with a spazzed-out V tach rhythm defibrillated into sinus rhythm. Made me laugh the first time I saw it.

A few seconds later, Dr. Chia popped out of the eye room, Purelling her hands.

An older nurse named Linda held up a notebook with two St. Joseph's stickers on them: "Your family-oriented hospital away from home" and "The heartbeat of Côte-des-Neiges." Before I could giggle to myself at their cheesiness, I tuned into what Linda was saying: "I don't wear my stethoscope when I have a psych patient."

She meant me. I stopped mid-step, in front of the exit doors between the ambulance and ambulatory side, near the old light boxes. They used to print X-rays and CT's and MRI's on actual film and hang them on this wall of opaque panels to illuminate them. Right now, I felt about as smart as these opaque panels.

"Me neither," Dr. Chia answered. "Not my first rodeo."

I flushed. Lori Goody hadn't been a psych patient. She'd been a drug-seeking patient with chest pain and palpitations. Was I not supposed to do a physical exam, even when a patient claimed she was having a heart attack?

"I've been kicked, I've been punched, I've had patients tried to strangle me. I don't wear my stethoscope to Code Whites anymore," said Kris, who'd joined us.

Then how do you listen to their hearts? I shouted in my head, but I was already mentally kicking myself.

I could have held my stethoscope in my hands as I advanced on LG. Why had I looped it around my neck? I found that position more comfortable, but what was more important, comfort or survival?

I could have kept my distance from her, monitoring her body language. As soon as she'd lunged at me, I could have darted away.

I could have asked for someone to come with me while I examined her, although that might have taken a good twenty minutes, given our almost non-existent night shift staff.

At the very least, I should have left the door open.

I'd had a few options. Bottom line, I hadn't been wary enough.

What the hell was wrong with me? It wasn't even the first time someone had tried to strangle me, although it was the first attempt with my own stethoscope.

"Oh, well. Maybe you won't have to wear your stethoscope at all soon, right, Val?" Kris said.

Huh? I knew that Dr. Chia's first name was Valerie, and I'd heard ultrasound called "the stethoscope of the 21st century," but none of us had given up stethoscopes completely. For one thing, we were always fighting over the few ultrasound machines, which seemed to be located on the opposite side of wherever I was working.

"I know *I'd* retire right away!" Roxanne chimed in. She'd rolled up behind us with her WOW.

"Better than getting walked out," muttered Julie, the little preposée, which is what they called orderlies in Montreal.

"And you don't even have to rip off drugs from the OR! Your million is *legal!*" Kris called, before Dr. Chia shushed her.

I felt like my hair was standing straight up from my head. Someone had stolen drugs from the OR? How'd I miss that memo?

But in more exciting news, Dr. Valerie Chia was a millionaire. Recently and legally. That meant...

"It's not me. It's Mark's, okay?" Dr. Chia typed on her WOW, trying to ignore them.

"He's your *conjoint.*" Kris used the French slang for partner. "You live with the guy. It's yours too. If he says anything else, you take him straight to a lawyer."

"She's already got one," Roxanne said, and Dr. Chia threw up her hands and asked the ceiling, "Are there no secrets around here?"

"Not a lot," said Kris. "What happened? He's already being a dick about it?"

"No, nothing like that. I just—I wanted him to claim it anony-mously. You can hire a lawyer to claim it. The lottery corporation wants photos of the winners. It's part of their conditions, but for privacy reasons, it's better not to do them."

"Of course," said Kris. "Not our first rodeo. But he wouldn't let you do the lawyer thing?"

"It was his ticket," said Dr. Chia.

"I saw your picture with him, though. It's right on Facebook!" said Roxanne.

Dr. Chia's shoulders sagged. "He really wanted me to be there. You know. Celebrate it together."

Strange. I regarded her with new eyes. Dr. Chia didn't have to slog in the ER, risking a boot to the face from Lori Goody. She could be at home, snuggling with her newly-minted millionaire common-law husband and glorying in her 1.2K Facebook likes!

It was strange to me that they weren't married, but I'm from the province of Ontario. In Quebec, people don't tend to marry as much. Something to do with rebelling against the church.

Man. If I were a millionaire, or as good as married to a millionaire...

My thoughts drifted to Tucker and me, him shirtless and sunburned on the beach, grinning as he handed me a fruity drink.

And there was Ryan sliding his arms around me from behind, kissing my shoulder.

Um. My turn to blush. Instead, I made a point of asking, "Do you mind if I give more Ativan to bed 14? I thought one or two milligrams IV."

"Oh, yes, I already told Roxanne to get it," said Dr. Chia, who had also turned red and started typing again. "I want 14 sedated. She might need a lot more. I think the order's in. Hang on." She clicked a few times. "Yes, there it is."

"I'm not seeing it. That's what I came to tell you," said Roxanne.

"Did you hit refresh?"

"Only a billion times. I'd take it as a verbal order, but you know we're not supposed to do that any more."

"I know. SARKET," Dr. Chia said, with loathing. "At this rate, Dave will finish his night shift before I compile my charts or get any orders in!" She started clicking. "There. Can you see that?"

"No. Hang on, I'll refresh. Again."

Meanwhile, I perked up. Dave meant Dr. Dave Dupuis, also known as God, because he heroically manages the worst cases, the busiest shifts, the craziest call karma. Things no one else gets at a relatively sleepy community hospital when all traumas are automatically diverted to UC, the University College Hospital.

Someone fell off a bridge?

Dave's on.

Someone pulled a knife?

Dave's on.

If I'm going to stay up 24/7 on a night shift, I'd rather learn from "God" and get some cool stories out of it than endure Dr. Callendar complaining that I hadn't spent 20 minutes thoroughly examining a pimple.

I couldn't resist whispering to Dr. Chia, "Congratulations."

"On what?" She yanked her head up from the screen to bind me with her dark eyes.

"Your partner winning the lottery."

Her cheeks reddened, and she avoided my eyes. "Thanks."

Clearly, she was embarrassed about the money and wanted everyone to ignore it. If I'd won the lottery, though, not only would I yell, "I'm king of the world!" and do a victory dance, I'd—well, I don't know if I'd abandon medicine, but I'd at least go home and take a good, long nap.

I suppressed a yawn. No time for sleep. Dr. Dupuis had already swept in through the doors beside the old light boxes and started signing over with the evening doctor.

This is the deal, as a resident. You work longer hours than the staff doctor. You start at 11, you finish at 8, and on weekdays, you have to go to teaching afterward. If you're very unlucky, you might have to *give* the teaching session at 0800, fielding questions on the epidemiology of measles in an age of idiotic anti-vaxxers, when you're so tired that you can barely figure out which way is the bathroom.

The staff doctor comes on at midnight and finishes at 7:30. Much more tidy. And you can bet your ass they skip teaching rounds afterward if their neurons aren't firing.

As I approached Dr. Dupuis, Dr. Callendar cut in front of me, already jabbering about bed 5.

I grimaced. Callendar never moves as fast as when he's finishing a shift.

"Walk with us, Hope." Dr. Dupuis gestured me toward them with a long, thin hand. He reminded me of a stork, all arms and legs and pale feathers (blond hair), more Bill Gates than Hollywood hunk, but "God" was my favourite doctor, bar none.

Dr. Callendar didn't pause in his narration as I caught up with them at bed 6. "...a 70-year-old asthmatic who came in with a sat of 89. I gave her three Ventolins and Atrovents."

I perked up. The vast majority of asthmatics turn around quickly. It's rare for them to desaturate. And you don't see elderly asthmatics. Many of them are children or, at most, in their fifties. Maybe pollution wasn't as bad back then, or maybe smoking and emphysema carry them away first.

"You got the X-ray?" Dr. Dupuis asked Dr. Callendar.

"Yes. No pneumonia."

"What about a D-dimer, a trop, or BNP?"

Dr. Dupuis was also thinking about a differential diagnosis, like a pulmonary embolus, heart attack, or congestive heart failure.

Dr. Callendar waved his hand. "You can add those if you choose. In bed 7..."

If Dr. Callendar had been a resident, he would have had his ass handed to him for doing slipshod work. But as a staff, he could almost literally wave his hand and say, "I leave this as an exercise to the reader," a line that Ryan and I used to joke about from math textbooks, and the other staff wouldn't bother him. They'd sigh and clean up after him.

Dr. Dupuis took the crappy handover as I would have, straight-faced and unsmiling, making a mental list of what he had to add in once Callendar got out of the way.

I took notes on a clipboard, which Dr. Dupuis recognized with a flick of an eyelid. I wasn't doing it to win brownie points, though. I wrote things down because I tend to get tired and forget which bed needs Tylenol on a night shift.

I hung back near the nursing station once we reached room 14. I didn't want Lori Goody to recognize me.

"Who's this?" said Dr. Dupuis, noting my hesitation.

"It's the one with the scalpel," I said, before Dr. Callendar could. "You probably heard about it on your way in. I'll let you two talk about this one."

"We can do it now," said Dr. Dupuis, facing Dr. Callendar. "What's the patient still doing here? Why didn't the police take her away, or at least port her up to psych? She shouldn't be in the same area as Dr. Sze."

"What're you gonna do about it, FIRE ME?" Lori Goody hollered.

Dr. Callendar shrugged and took a step backwards, receding from Lori Goody's hearing range. "You know how it is. No psych beds, and the police are overwhelmed. They'll take her away as soon as possible."

"She shouldn't be in the same area as Dr. Sze," Dr. Dupuis repeated, and turned to our nurse, Roxanne. "What can we do about this?"

"Call the Glen," she said. "That's her sector."

So the patient was already known to psych and had been assigned to the new superhospital.

Dr. Callendar wrinkled his forehead. "I put a call out, and they never answered."

"Keep calling," said Dr. Dupuis. "You can't have an attacker and victim in the same area. It's not safe. How come there's no police, or even a security guard, at the door?"

I squiggled inside. I didn't want to be known as a victim, and I didn't want people to think they had to stand up for me. I could take care of myself.

On the other hand, it was nice to have people take charge after you got the crap kicked out of you, and Callendar got away with too much. Dr. Dupuis had let the clinical errors slide, knowing he'd fix them afterward, but he was pulling definite rank to protect me.

Roxanne gave me a slight wink.

The corner of my mouth lifted up. She really was one of my favourite nurses.

"I'm on my way out," said Dr. Callendar, glancing at the clock, but he snapped at the secretary, "Get me the Glen. What have you been waiting for?" like it was all her fault.

I knew he hadn't bothered pushing them to transfer Lori Goody out because, unlike Dr. Dupuis, he couldn't care less about me. Seriously, for him, I ranked lower than smegma. But Dr. Callendar was on his way out, in more ways than one.

I'd rather work a night shift with Dupuis than a day shift with Callendar.

"Call the police too," said Dr. Callendar. "Get everyone. I haven't got all day!"

Dr. Dupuis ignored him. "Start seeing patients, Hope," he said, and I grabbed a chart, happy to return to work and avoid the drama.

Dr. Dupuis plucked the next two charts without checking the chief complaints. "Let's motor. The paramedics had six overdoses tonight already, and they're running low on Narcan." He shook his head.

Narcan was amazing. I saw one patient go from complete coma to sitting up in bed, trying to take a swing at us, thanks to the narcotic antidote.

Six overdoses before midnight was a lot. Way more than I'd ever heard of.

"How come we're running out?" I managed to ask. "'Cause of the drips?" Narcan's antidote effect wears off. You often have to give more than one dose, and then an infusion. I felt for the paramedics. While you're saving one person's life, you give whatever it takes. But when the next call comes in, and the next call, and the next, you can run out of Narcan. And then, like Kris pointed out, their only option is to ship them to the ER.

"That's part of it," agreed Dr. Dupuis. "Brace yourself. But in the meantime, let's work on the patients here and now." He pointed at the computer.

Between Lori Goody and Alyssa Taylor, plus the evening rush,

SARKET kindly showed us that our wait time had ballooned up to 14 hours. Some patients would leave when it got too late, or they'd waited too long, but not most of them. It was like the world's worst Disneyworld.

"I need to transfer a psych patient. Stat! She attacked one of our doctors!" Dr. Callendar bellowed.

I shook my head. He loved to throw his weight around. He hadn't bothered until Dr. Dupuis leaned on him and he was raring to go home, but at least now he was doing his job.

"You can lock her up tonight, for all I care," Dr. Callendar shouted. "As long as you get her out of here!"

I moved around him to grab my pen, which I'd forgotten on the other end of the nursing station.

"Yes, it was a resident doctor. You can talk to her directly if you want. The patient tried to strangle her with her own stethoscope and then stab her with a scalpel!"

I winced as I tiptoed to room 12, which was perilously close to room 14.

"We take the health of our staff very seriously. No one deserves to be attacked in her workplace," intoned Dr. Callendar.

Ye gads. What a hypocrite. Next he'd post on Instagram under #metoo.

I checked my phone for the time: 00:25. No messages from Tucker or anyone else.

Alyssa's Taylor's results should be brewing. After I saw a few patients, I'd track down her boyfriend and figure out exactly who had tried to break her face.

7

B ed 12's clipboard chart gave his name, his health card number, birth date, and triage diagnosis, BLOODY DIARRHEA.

I'd forgotten to bring a workstation on wheels, or WOW, so I didn't have the guy's triage history or vital signs. I'd have to wing it and bring my computer next time. WOW's didn't fit into the ambulatory rooms, but the ambulance side's curtains would expand to accommodate them.

"Are you the doctor?" The 23-year-old white guy sat on the edge of his bed, texting on his phone. He didn't look too agonized.

Neither did his buddy, who turned off his own phone and smiled at me. Even sitting down, I could tell that he was taller, broader, and better-looking than the patient, and he knew it.

I flashed them both a generic smile. "Yes, I'm the resident doctor, Dr. Sze. You can pronounce it like the letter C."

"I need the police here now!" said Dr. Callendar.

"Fuck the police!" Lori Goody answered.

I started asking Bed 12 his history in as loud a voice as I could manage, trying to drown out both of them. Of course it was abdominal pain with bloody diarrhea, and the patient had zero interest in a rectal exam.

"What?" he said.

"You know. A finger in the bum to check for bloody stool."

The patient paled and glanced at his friend.

"Bloody poo," I explained. My job is so glamourous.

"You can't do that!" he yelped.

I nodded solemnly. Not only can I do that, but I do it often, although perhaps not well.

"I don't do stuff like that!"

"You don't have to do anything. Either lie on the bed on your side with your knees bent, or drop your pants and underwear and lean over the bed." I demonstrated how to do the latter, legs apart and butt in the air, although less enthusiastically than if he hadn't been a guy a few years younger than me. How embarrassin'.

"I can't," he protested.

His friend guffawed. "It's part of the deal, buddy. That's why you came here, right? To get checked out." He winked at me.

"No way!"

"Oh, man, I'm so glad this is you and not me." His friend literally bent in half, he was laughing so hard.

"I can't. Seriously, I can't. Can't you write that I refused or something?"

"I guess you could give stool specimens," I said. "But if you're actively bleeding right now—"

"I'm not! It was yesterday!"

"Then why did you come in today?" I eyeballed his friend. They were talking like straight guys, but I couldn't assume anything. "Was it after some sexual activity, using toys or body parts?" My neck flushed. That was as tactful as I could get.

"No. Hell, no. Oh, my God. I want to die. Seriously. Just kill me now."

I changed the subject. "Is there a history of Crohn's or Ulcerative Colitis in your family?"

"What's that?"

"It's Inflammatory Bowel Disease."

"Yeah, I think my aunt has that."

I couldn't get too excited yet. "Not *Irritable* Bowel Syndrome, or IBS. It has to be *inflammatory,* which is Crohn's Disease or Ulcerative Colitis."

"Um, yeah, I think so. I'm not sure. I'll text my mom."

"You do that." A second degree relative wasn't the be all and end all. It might increase the likelihood that it wasn't only a garden variety infectious diarrhea, although I'd cover those bases with stool cultures.

I gave him a quick physical exam, sans rectal exam ("Please don't do that. Seriously. I'd rather die"), and headed back to the nursing station to start my interminable charting, reminding myself to type, "Rectal exam refused."

SARKET took a long time to load even simple things like our basic order sets. While its wheels spun, I checked my phone.

Nothing from Tucker.

Ryan's mom, Mrs. Wu, hadn't called back or texted. Her first name was Cheryl, but I'd never called her that, and she'd never invited me to. Ryan and I started dating pre-med, when I wasn't used to calling adults by their first names. Mrs. Wu had suited both of us fine.

Then I remembered my Finding Friends app. After Tucker introduced me to it, Ryan had reluctantly joined, but deleted himself from my Finding Friends list after he blocked my phone numbers, Skype, FaceTime, Facebook, Twitter (I don't even really use Twitter!), Snapchat, Whatsapp, Line, and probably other stuff I didn't even know because Ryan was the engineer and much more techno-adept than me.

I brought up Finding Friends anyway. All I needed was his last location. At least that would show me something.

Tucker was driving west, toward Ottawa.

No Ryan Wu showed up anywhere. Of course.

Ryan's best friend was this guy named Terry Goh. I liked him, but they always talked about things I don't care about, like running, video games, or worst of all, church.

I took a deep breath and texted Terry.

Hey. You seen Ryan lately? His mom's looking for him.

There. That didn't sound too ex-girlfriendy, although it was awfully late to be bugging him.

Screw that. I was awake and hunting for Ryan.

After a minute, I copied and pasted that message to every one of Ryan's friends in my contacts, which was a whopping six of them, but oh, well. He mostly made friends at church, so we didn't have many in common, and when Ryan and I wanted to be alone, we wanted to be Alone, if you know what I mean.

Still, I felt a pang. It made it easier for us to split up that we didn't have friends in common. That was less traumatic, so yay? Except that I still wanted to talk about him, still wanted to remember him, still regretted not having him in my life every day.

After a pause, I decided to call Ryan myself. Even if it was futile and I was a jerk calling after midnight.

It rang straight through to voice mail. Not even half a ring. He'd blocked me.

I texted him.

Where are you? Your mom's worried.

After a pause, I typed,

I love you, Ryan.

You're never supposed to say stuff like that. It makes it harder for your ex to separate from you. You're supposed to rip the other person away, like a Band Aid, because repeated reminders are too cruel.

But he was missing. What if something happened to him? What if it was one of the murderers I'd put away? They could ask a friend to whack him, or hire a hitman. Chances were, they hadn't gotten the memo that I'd switched boyfriends and could easily decide it was a good idea to chomp on Ryan.

That was crazy talk.

On the other hand, I'd met too many psychopaths to dismiss the possibility.

I finished my orders and called the Ottawa Police.

8

The Ottawa Police number was automated voice mail hell. I could see why they'd invented 911, because otherwise you'd grow old and die before you talked to a human being.

On the upside, I didn't have to feel guilty about calling a machine in the wee hours of the morning.

On the downside, zero people would answer me or take me seriously. I did manage to leave a message, but by the time any human listened to it, I'd be asleep post-shift and/or incoherent with insomnia.

"What've you got for me, Hope?"

I jumped. Dr. Dupuis had rolled up in the chair next to me. Somehow, I always managed to pick the defective chair that sank down to toddler size as soon as I rested my bum on it, so he towered over me even more than usual.

I reviewed the bloody diarrhea case.

"His heart rate was 110," Dr. Dupuis said, clicking to the triage note and pointing at the vital sign highlighted in red.

Oh, no. Usually, I reviewed vital signs first thing. The lack of electronic record had thrown me off my game. The patient must have been triaged to the ambulance side for tachycardia as a sign of hemorrhage. "He was anxious," I said, because stress also ups your heart rate. "He kept asking me not to do the rectal exam."

"Still, better keep an eye on the CBC."

"I ordered one! And a group and type, INR, and the SMA-7." My face burned. "Usually, I circle any abnormal vitals on the paper chart. Sorry."

Dr. Dupuis nodded. "I noticed that."

Of course he had. God noticed everything. I fumbled with the keyboard, adding a normal saline bolus. I could give him ringer's lactate, but the studies hadn't shown a big difference between the two, especially for young patients with normal kidneys. "I'll give him a litre and see if he responds. If his hemoglobin is low, I'll repeat it—"

"And usually," he continued, "patients don't try to strangle you and stab you with a scalpel. We're having trouble moving that patient from room 14, as you may have heard. You want to go home?"

Confusion exploded in my brain. Of course I wanted to go home and sleep like a normal human being. But was that wimping out? My voice felt a little less hoarse already. I could push through another 7 plus hours.

Dr. Dupuis watched me.

He was the first person who'd showed me compassion. Well, Roxanne had been nice to me. Everyone else thought it was my own fault for wearing my stethoscope.

I rubbed my eyes, willing away any tears. Yes, I wanted to go home and look for Ryan.

No, I couldn't afford to miss any more work. They kept threatening to hold me back a month or two if I missed any more clinical time.

"Look. Take a break." Dr. Dupuis pursed his thin lips. "Even if you go lie down in the back room for a few minutes. I don't want you working right now. You've started this patient, you're bolusing him, the labs won't be back for an hour or two. You're off for at least half an hour, or until I get room 14 cleared. Got that?"

I still hesitated.

"Go."

He was serious. I stood up. The chair seat tried to rebound but couldn't.

Dr. Dupuis gave me a crooked grin and pointed to the resident's room. The hallway to both the sleep rooms, mine and the staff's, hid between bed 9 and 10.

Obediently, I plucked the key from the Plexiglass window's ledge above the secretary's desk. They kept the key attached to a two-foot long stick painted yellow to make sure sleepy residents didn't wander away with it.

"Good job," said Dr. Dupuis, scooping up the next three charts.

He could work faster without me. Having a learner meant stopping to teach. Without me, he could simultaneously blaze through the patients in the waiting room, fix Dr. Callendar's patients, take sign over for Dr. Chia's patients, and handle a shark attack coming through the door. He was like the Olympic gold medallist in emergency medicine.

I sighed to myself. Would I ever be that good? Especially if I was hamstrung by patients trying to murder me every other second?

I passed the mini kitchen on the right, unlocked the resident's room on the left, and dropped into bed, mind blank, too tired to brush my teeth.

God told me to rest, so I should rest. Thus spake the Lord.

But my mind whirled.

Ryan.

Tucker's on him

Tucker.

Tucker's not in danger.

But he had surgery times two, and now he's out driving all night. How smart is that?

I got up and texted Tucker. *If you're too tired, pull over and sleep. I don't want to lose you. I love you.*

No answer, but he wouldn't answer if he was driving, and Ottawa was a two hour drive away, even if you hadn't worked all day and evening.

Ah, God. I couldn't rest. I sat up.

There was only one thing I could work on right now, and that was Alyssa Taylor's case. Since she refused to talk to me, I'd worm the truth out of her boyfriend, Patrick Warren.

I couldn't let Dr. Dupuis know I was disobeying his direct orders to rest, so I took the back way out. Instead of retreading past his room and the kitchen into the acute area of the emerg and taking a left out the door with the old light boxes, I ducked out the back door of the residents' room, directly into the hall.

This way, I could circle outside the ER, secretly making my way to the front doors, the main entrance where a lone security guard usually sat at night. Sure enough, I spotted some beefy white guy who wasn't Patrick Warren, so I migrated back to check the guard by the emerg entrance.

No Patrick. I found the older man, the sixtyish guy who'd attended the Code White.

"Hi," he said. His brown eyes seemed to miss nothing behind his glasses. "Everything okay in there?"

"Not too bad, thanks, uh, Charles." I'd glanced at his security badge, which said CHARLES PACKARD. I tried to call adults by their first names nowadays, but my cheeks reddened. "I was hoping to talk to one of your colleagues, Patrick. Is he going back to the front desk?" The front desk guard seemed to act as hospital locating after hours, meaning that when I tried to page, say, the internal medicine consultant, my own pager started beeping, and I had to dial the guard back to tell him, *No,* I'm *the* resident. *I'm not trying to phone myself. Call the big guns.*

"Patrick? He's doing rounds," said Charles Packard.

I blinked. Guards strolled the hallways, but I'd never consciously realized that they'd be patrolling more often than not. "Oh, okay. I only have a few minutes. Do you know where he is?"

"I can give him a message. Your name is?" He clicked open a ball-point pen, a piece of paper at the ready.

"No, I need to speak to him directly. Could you talk to him on your radio or something? I can meet him somewhere."

Charles Packard frowned. "He's on duty right now. He shouldn't be interrupted."

"You know what? Never mind." Patrick had missed work to bring Alyssa in. I was probably getting the guy in trouble with his boss right now. It reminded me of my own life, being on probation for missed work. Yet another similarity between us.

It belatedly occurred to me that Alyssa would have Patrick's phone number, and I could contact him through her. No need for the boss to know anything.

Slipping into room 13 meant I'd risk being seen by Dr. Dupuis—and Lori Goody. But I'd have to take that risk.

"You know what? It's fine. I'll see him when I see him. Thanks, Charles."

"No problem, Dr. Sze."

For a second, I wondered how he knew my name. Then I realized I was wearing my badge, and for once, it was facing the right way around. I wasn't the only one sleuthing in this hospital.

I should have felt comforted, since it was his job to be alert and identify wrongdoing, but I couldn't smile.

I hurried back to the ER, trying to figure out the most unobtrusive way to get back in without alerting Dr. Dupuis. The conference room was my best bet, but of course it was locked from the outside. We don't want anyone breaking into the ER from the hallway.

I'd have to sneak in through one of the main doors. I pondered the layout again.

I usually took the doors next to the old light boxes, between the acute and ambulatory side. I liked hitting the buttons to make them open automatically, but it created a ruckus because we brought stretchers through there. People glanced up to see who was coming in.

I could either cut through triage and patient registration and sneak in the hall between the eye room and resus, or cut between the four ambulatory examining rooms, but that would put me back within eyeshot of Charles Packard, and I already felt stupid enough without underlining the fact that I couldn't re-enter the ER without trying twice.

Worse, the ambulatory side increased the risk that I might run into Dr. Dupuis as he shot around the ER, seeing ten million patients at once, like the doctor equivalent of the Indian god with all the arms.

Hmm. Humiliation vs. God's ire. Decisions, decisions.

I marched away from Charles Packard, chose the doors at the light boxes, and took a sharp right to room 13.

There was no sound from Lori Goody. Either she'd been successfully drugged or ported out or both.

My shoulders relaxed. When I glanced down at the stretcher, in the dim light, Alyssa Taylor stared back at me.

"Hi," I whispered.

She blinked in response.

"I'm looking for Patrick. Do you know where he is, or could you text him?"

She held up her phone and typed furiously.

I can't find him.

She couldn't move from her stretcher. Then it clicked in my foggy brain. "Oh. You mean that you've been texting him already?"

She started to nod and stopped herself as the edge of the collar reminded her to stay still. She showed me her phone's messages to him.

HB

CRB

WRU

I'm not so into abbreviations like that—I vaguely pieced together that WRU probably meant Where are you—but I noted the times. She'd been texting him steadily from 23:53 until 01:05.

He'd answered at 00:06.

ily rounding parking lot brb

Emojis at 00:23, 00:30, 00:33.

Then nothing.

Even I knew, and sometimes used, BRB for Be Right Back. So what happened to Patrick?

Presumably he was patrolling the hospital. But which part? It was weird that Patrick had texted frequently, and then not at all for half an hour.

Patrick knew his beloved was bedbound, beaten, and scared. Even if he'd been called away to work, he'd try to answer her.

The words fell out of my mouth. "I'll go find him."

9

Before I left Alyssa, I asked for Patrick's number. She sent me everything. Cell, Whatsapp, Snapchat, Insta, Facebook messenger, e-mail, home address, everything. Plus she mouthed, "Thank you."

It was a 180 degree shift in attitude from *No.*

That worried me, too.

When I exited room 13, I spotted Dr. Dupuis's green scrub-clad back blocking the corridor to both our call rooms and the conference room. He was probably heading to the tiny kitchen nook tucked into the right, in front of the staff call room.

It meant I couldn't retrieve my coat and mittens from my call room, so I retreated back toward the ambulatory zone.

Did I have to go outside? Patrick had rounded in the parking lot an hour ago. He'd be long gone by now.

But maybe I could follow his boot prints.

No, there would be too many people coming in and out of the hospital, even after midnight.

What were the chances I could roam around the hospital and find him? St. Joe's wasn't massive like the Glen "superhospital," but it was still sizeable for one person to investigate every corridor.

I decided to pop outside for a quick look immediately around the building. Not the smartest idea in January in Canada, wearing only my scrubs, but I always packed multiple layers underneath, including fleece, because I was perpetually cold. A night shift cranked that up another order of magnitude. Once, a menopausal nurse told me that just looking at me, all bundled up with a fake fur hoodie, gave her a hot flash.

"What are you doing, Hope?" a woman's voice called.

I jumped.

Dr. Chia stared at me from the ambulatory desk. "Didn't Dr. Dupuis tell you to take a break or go home? We're worried about you."

"Yeah. Thanks. I'm, ah, getting fresh air."

"It's minus 25 out there," she said, wrinkling her nose.

"I know. I'll only be a second. As soon as I get some wind on my face, I'll feel better."

"Panic attack?"

"What?" Ye gads. I'd never mentioned my PTSD to her. All the staff doctors must've talked about me and Tucker, the post-traumatic twins. Was it better for her to think I was a psych patient, or disobeying them? Decisions, decisions. "I need some fresh air," I repeated. I'm a terrible liar. Best to keep it simple.

She moved her mouse. "This stupid computer is frozen. Well, anyway, take my lab coat."

I doubted it would help much. "I'll be fine—"

"Hope." She stood up and plucked her white coat off her chair. "It's not much, but it's better than nothing."

In her own way, she was trying to protect me. Maybe she was making up for the whole "not my first rodeo" conversation. So I took it. It was warm, and it smelled a bit flowery, like her. "Thanks."

"You're welcome." She had already moved on to another computer and was logging in, trying to get her charting done so that she could go home.

Her white coat was a denser weave than the standard St. Joe's issue polyester. It might protect a bit against the wind.

Maybe when I was making the big bucks, I'd spring for a coat like this.

I buttoned it all the way, which only brought it up to my collarbone, with a V of neck skin exposed. Then I tucked my head down against the wind as I headed out the emergency room door, past triage and patient reg and Charles Packard.

This time, I had no choice in exits. They locked the other doors after hours, to divert all foot traffic through the ER. It's a safety thing, to force everyone to pass by the security guard.

The wind slapped me in the face, slid down my collar, up the coat's hem, and between the buttons.

I squinted as my eyes adjusted to the night, lit only by some street lamps.

No ambulances squatted by the door. Most of the cars were parked in the lot behind the hospital and around the Annex building, to my right.

I glanced down at the snow, but there were too many tracks leading in and out.

On the other hand, relatively few would lead to the parking lot and immediately circle back again. Most people would either park and walk in and wait to be seen, or there'd be a few drop offs. I'd look for a pair of men's boot prints making a circle.

All that would prove was that Patrick had made the rounds, of course. Unless he was still out here.

I shivered. My breath made clouds in the frosty air.

This was dumb. I should go in and lie down like at least two doctors had commanded.

Instead, I took a step into the night, examining various boot prints.

Once, my favourite police officer, Officer Visser gave me an impromptu talk on tracking people's prints. She told me that when you run, your shoes make deeper impressions at the heel and toe. Your shoes also sink more deeply into the ground or snow if you're carrying a heavy load, like a dead body.

I hadn't noticed the kind of shoes Patrick was wearing. If pressed,

I'd say they were black and heavy-looking. And he had above average-sized feet as well, maybe size 12.

I turned the light on my phone, shining at the snow. We'd had a snow fall that evening. Light flakes were still coming down, but I had a good view of the tracks.

One of them had a good, solid, man-sized tread—you'd need good soles, as a security guard—that headed toward the parking lot. It was a long shot, but I started to follow the tracks. They seemed to have the same stride length and an even depth, so I didn't think he'd been running. Or carrying a dead body.

It was cold enough that my skin hurt, and I had to blink against the snow.

I thought I heard something and twisted my head diagonally to the right, scanning the silent cars lined up in the parking lot ahead of me, layered in snow.

Nothing. I started walking and heard it again, this time behind me. Tap, tap, tap.

Footsteps. Had Patrick somehow circled around me? I twisted to the left now, even though most of the street lamps were straight ahead and to my right, in the parking lot, or behind me, at the ER entrance.

"Patrick!" The chill air rushed down my open mouth and throat, making me cough.

I spotted only a black blur of an arm and a boot before someone pinned my arms to my sides in a bear hug from behind. "Got 'er."

He reeked of marijuana smoke. I opened my mouth to scream. I was right beside the hospital, maybe 40 feet from the ER entrance. Not in direct view of the glass doors, but close by.

Someone would see. Someone would hear.

Before I could do more than suck air, a dirty glove clapped against my mouth.

lyssa's broken face blazed into my mind. Was this how it started? Was someone terrorizing all the women around St. Joe's?

No fuckin' way.

I stomped on the black boot, trying to shatter the foot. Harder to break in a boot, but not impossible.

The shock of impact shot up to my hip.

All he did was grunt. Didn't even lift up his foot. But his arms loosened a smidge.

I managed to jerk my pointy right elbow backward, slamming him in the gut.

He gave an oof, faint but unmistakable.

I swung back toward the ER. A few steps would do it. At least I'd be in the light. The guard and maybe a patient would spot me.

"Grab her!"

That was a different voice. There were two of them, tag teaming me before I'd gotten more than two steps.

A hand snapped through the air, cuffing my right wrist. My dominant wrist.

I tried to shake it off. He yanked me toward him like my arm was a fishing line.

I screamed through the foggy darkness, a raw noise that pierced the night, but weak because I'd already been almost strangled tonight.

The snow descended, clogging my eyelashes behind my glasses. I couldn't see well, I was alone, I was underdressed, but damned if I would let them have me.

I screamed again, even raspier than before, and kicked the one clamping my wrist. I didn't make contact, but it kept him at bay for a second before he lunged again, tackling me around the waist. Then he began to drag me backward.

Don't let them get you in a car. If they get you in a car, you're dead.

A whistle punctured my thoughts. It Dopplered from the sidewalk, ten times louder than my screams, and a woman's voice shouted, "Let her go!"

The attacker dropped me.

I slipped on the icy asphalt and barely caught myself, my right arm skidding sideways as I landed on my hip and bare hand.

I scrambled to my feet, wary of getting pinned on the ground, but two dark shapes raced away from the street, toward the parking lot—where I thought Patrick had gone—and out of sight.

A couple approached me from the sidewalk. The woman wore a beige head scarf and a long parka. She was the one who stretched her hands out to me and said, "Are you all right?"

"Yes," I gasped. My word made a cloud in the air.

The husband, who was larger than her, scanned for my attackers. He spoke to her in their language. She shook her head.

"Let's get you inside," said the woman. "My husband will call the police. Don't worry."

Can't worry. Running. I bolted for the door while she shielded my back and the husband brought up the rear, already murmuring on his phone.

Warm air blasted us as the automatic doors flared open. My glasses fogged up worse, but I was lucky I was still wearing them.

My arm smarted. My biceps had been over-stretched breaking my fall. My right ankle was tender, too, but I could tell it wasn't broken because it could bear my weight, even though I'd already sprained it twice last month.

My throat ached, but I had to talk. Again. "Thank you," I whispered.

I checked for the security guard, but Charles Packard chatted further down the hall, helping a family by the vending machine.

I rolled my eyes. The one time I needed a security guard, he'd left his post. Murphy's Law should be renamed the Hope Sze Universal Commandment.

I turned back to my saviours. "Were you coming here?"

She shook her head. "Just walking home."

"Did you see them?"

She shook her head again. "It was too dark. They were wearing black. But my husband is very observant. He'll describe them to the police."

I wished I had her confidence. Telling the cops that two black blobs had attacked me wouldn't get us further than "uh huh."

My teeth began to chatter.

The woman wrapped her arm around me. "Are you all right?"

I nodded, although I clearly wasn't.

"You want to see the doctor?"

I half-laughed, even though it hurt my throat. "I *am* the emergency doctor. Well, I'm one of the resident doctors, Dr. Sze."

"Oh, that's why you have that coat." She looked down at it, clearly confused by the embroidery. "But—you're Dr. Valerie—" She didn't dare pronounce the last name.

I glanced down at my front pocket. "I borrowed this jacket from Dr. Valerie Chia, the evening doctor. It's not mine."

"Are you all right, then?"

"Much better, thanks to you two. We'll all have to talk to the police." I was afraid they'd take off and leave me trying to explain what had happened, with my broken voice.

"No problem," said the man, in quite good English. He nodded, squarely meeting my eyes.

My shoulders relaxed. They weren't going anywhere. Two strangers had saved me and would continue to save me.

He pulled the phone away from his head to look at his wife, then at me. "It's strange, but they say the police are already at St. Joe's. In the emergency room."

I nodded and gave him the thumbs up, too tired to explain that either they must have arrived to carry away Lori Goody, to interview me, or both. I'd have to head back in and face Dr. Dupuis's wrath for taking off and nearly getting kidnapped.

"Is this a very dangerous hospital?" asked the woman, gently patting my shoulder. "I don't know if you should work here."

I chuckled. St. Joe's was considered a snoozy community hospital before I arrived.

The man said something in their language, and her eyes widened. "This is the one with the hostage taking! Oh my goodness. We moved here from Toronto and didn't realize. Oh, my."

Crap. The last thing I needed was her fleeing in terror. I slipped my phone out of my front pocket—somehow, I'd managed to keep it on me—and wrote, *It's usually safe. Welcome.*

"We're not scared," said the man, reading my thoughts. I must have looked agonized. "Let's go talk to the police."

Dr. Dupuis stood by the secretary's desk on the acute side, red-faced and the angriest I'd ever seen him. He watched us walk past the eye room and resus area into the nearest opening to the nursing station, which was, unfortunately, right in front of him. He barely glanced at my saviours, focusing on me. "Where were you."

The man said, "This poor doctor was attacked in the parking lot. Two men tried to drag her off. I called the police. Are they here?"

On cue, two officers loomed behind Dr. Dupuis. One of them flipped open a notebook as soon as he saw me. The other stared.

"The police are here to interview you about the patient in 14. What's this about two men in the parking lot?" said Dr. Dupuis.

I typed on my phone, *It's true. I tried to find the security guard in the parking lot, and two men attacked me.*

I let the couple explain the rest, which resulted in two officers interviewing me in the conference room before they'd talk to the couple. At least it got me away from Dr. Dupuis.

Before I left, I took the woman's hand in mine and mouthed to her and her husband, "Thank you." I didn't even know their names.

"I'll pray for you," she said.

Well, Ryan wasn't praying for me any more. I'd take it. "Thank you," I mouthed again, as the police led me away.

11

My wooden chair creaked as I sat at the Formica conference table with the police, struggling to describe the two men in black.

"How big were they?" asked the cop who was writing my testimony in a pocket-sized blue notebook. He was younger and a bit chubby, like Seth Rogan, minus the humour.

"Bigger than me," I said, closing my eyes to try and picture the scene. This insulated me from their stares and the overhead fluorescent light, but it made me sleepy. I pried my eyelids open and blinked at them.

"How much bigger?" asked the fortyish cop. His salt and pepper hair was so close-cropped, it looked painful. Maybe that was why he looked annoyed with life in general. Well, that and the fact that it was nearly 2 a.m. He took a sip of the coffee Andrea had placed in front of him.

"Um, at least 5 foot 7. Maybe up to 6 feet?" I shifted in my chair, scraping it on the tile floor. The sound echoed around the cavernous conference room.

Salt 'n' Pepa made a face.

It's lame, but when most adults are taller than you, I only have a few categories of size. Teeny (much shorter than me). Normal (within a few inches of my size, which is five foot two and a quarter). Tall (anyone over 5 foot nine). I suppose I could make a category for extra-tall, but I don't really notice unless it hurts my neck to look up. I'm not like a guy constantly comparing size to see if I measure up.

"Wider than me," I said, which might not have seemed like such a help, because I'm on the narrow side, but I held my hands out. Even with the puffy coat, at least one of the guys, the one who'd grabbed me, had been stocky. "Up to 200 pounds. Definitely over 160. Let's say 190."

Salt 'n' Pepa raised his eyebrows, but I have to be more precise with weight because we dose drugs accordingly. I'm not super talented at it, like some of the nurses, but I can guesstimate weight a bit better.

"That's the one who grabbed you?" asked Young 'n' Chubby.

"Yup. I never saw the other one, just heard him. But they were both men." I hesitated. "From the voices, I don't think they were old. Like, not elderly. Say between 18 and 50, more likely 20 to 35."

Salt 'n' Pepa sighed. I didn't take offence. He'd probably rather be out chasing down the suspects than taking vague testimony. On the other hand, he had to get better at eliciting information from witnesses, or there'd be no one to chase if criminals didn't do the do right in front of his nose.

"As for race..."

Both of them leaned forward now, suddenly alert. Racial profiling isn't in vogue, but everyone does it.

"...I'm not sure. I was grabbed from behind, so I couldn't see the grabber's skin, and I never saw the other one properly. They didn't have any noticeable accents. Well, one of them might have been French." French accents are so ubiquitous that they barely register on me. I tilted my head, closing my eyes. "The leader—the one not doing the grabbing—could have had a slight French accent, but I can't swear to it."

Young 'n' Chubby tapped his pen on the paper and glanced at his partner, who sighed.

"Maybe the other witnesses can describe them better. I did stomp on the one who was holding me." Personally, I thought it was more impressive that I'd escaped being thrown in a car trunk and driven away.

"Did you see any hair?" said Salt 'n' Pepa.

I shook my head. "He was wearing a hat. He kept it on the whole time."

"Did he have a beard, or any facial hair?"

"I don't know." I felt silly, but he'd pinned me facing outward, and then I was trying to run, and my glasses fogged up. My eyes, always my weakest link, hadn't been able to see much. "He was wearing a black parka, though. Made out of tough, artificial material, like nylon. I think he was wearing it on his legs, too. Snow pants. And he had black boots on."

Young 'n' Chubby wrote it down unenthusiastically. Black, black, black clothes that the perp could have already trashed, and he'd only grabbed me instead of raping me, beating me, and/or killing me. Yawn.

"Just one more thing," I said. "I was wearing Dr. Chia's lab coat, with her name on the front. It's really distinctive because of the rhythm strip on the back. You know, part of an electrocardiogram, moving from ventricular fibrillation to sinus rhythm—"

They stared at me like I was speaking Martian.

"Anyway, she's the only doctor with a coat like that. Everyone else has regular lab coats." Some emergency residents wore black zip-ups with that same rhythm strip, but you wouldn't mix up a white lab coat and a black jacket, so I left that out. "My point is, I don't know if they grabbed me because they were after me, or Dr. Chia, or a random woman. They didn't say anything besides 'Got her' and 'Grab her.'" I couldn't repress a shiver. Even though I was physically okay, no harm, no foul, it freaked me out to imagine what they might have planned for me.

"Why would they want to hurt you in particular?" said Young.

Salt tutted and said in French, "She's the famous one. The doctor who catches criminals. How many times?" he asked me, in English.

"There were six different cases," I said, not bothering to explain that sometimes I'd uncovered multiple crimes within each case.

Salt nodded. "Yes, but was there anything that made you think it might have been because of revenge, or..."

"No. That's what I'm telling you. They could have mistaken me for the other doctor, or a random woman to torture. I don't know. But I wanted to tell you that they could have been trying to kidnap Dr. Chia when they saw the lab coat."

They both stared at me in confusion.

I sighed. "Never mind."

"Okay," said Young. "It's too bad you couldn't get more description, but we'll talk to the couple. Let us know if you think of anything." They passed me their cards.

"Thanks. Were you already here for the patient who choked me with my stethoscope and threatened me with a scalpel?"

They nodded. Young 'n' Chubby's pen scratched across a new page.

"The patient in room 14 wanted a refill on her narcotics. When I told her I couldn't refill her prescription prematurely, she choked me with my stethoscope." I opened the lab coat and my fleece to show them the bruises. I could feel the energy in the room pick up. Finally, physical evidence that I'd been assaulted. Yay. "I ran out of the room, and she chased me with a scalpel, you know, the knives we use for surgery."

Salt perked up. "Did she cut you?"

"No, I got away before she could. Those things are sharp, you know." I imagined her driving it between my ribs, incising my heart. I'd be dead within minutes. St. Joe's doesn't have a trauma surgeon, and I don't think the general surgeon is in house at night. The closest one might be half an hour away.

An ER doctor would have to crack the chest to stopper up the hole, and probably no one but Dr. Dupuis would consider it. "But she did choke me with my stethoscope." I hadn't had a chance to check myself for bruises, so I felt along my throat and turned my head to the side to give them a better view. "See?"

They exchanged glances again. "You'll have to come to the station to have photos taken, if you want to press charges against the patient."

"I want to press charges," I said firmly. A nurse who'd been choked by a male patient, using her stethoscope, had said in a podcast interview, *I was trying not to hurt him. I was trying to knock his arms away. Instead, I should have grabbed a pen and tried to stab his eyeballs.*

Sounds harsh, but we've been so trained not to hurt anyone that we're the ones who almost get killed. We have to put a stop to it. Hence my squishing of Lori Goody's eyeball.

"Come to the station in the morning," they repeated.

If it bleeds, it leads. But if you don't bleed, if you're only bruised and seized, they don't care as much. They were certainly more interested in me being carted away in the parking lot than in arresting the patient in room 14.

"But she's right here"—if she hadn't been ported to the Glen —"and you're right here. You could lay charges on her right now. You could take her away with you."

Young cop exchanged glances with Salt. "We'll talk to her. We'll see about escorting her to the Glen."

I didn't like the sound of "we'll see." It wasn't a promise. But I tried honey instead of vinegar, firing up the "we're all in together" meme. "I appreciate that. I know you're on the night shift, and you're understaffed. Thank you."

They both nodded. Cops and emerg try to help each other out, as evinced by the coffee cooling on the table in front of them.

"Thanks on behalf of all women in this neighbourhood," I said, and I remembered Alyssa. "Did you know there was a woman who looks like someone tried to pulp her face and choke her?"

Salt 'n' Pepa stood up, not-so-subtly signalling an end to our conversation. "No. No one has reported it."

Young glanced up at him, his pen hesitating over his notebook.

I leaned forward, trying to make eye contact with Young. "Right. She wasn't willing to say anything. But the injuries are suspicious for assault."

"Well, then, contact us when you have evidence or when she's ready to report it," said Salt, still standing.

Young flipped his notebook closed.

I wasn't satisfied with that, but they were probably already overwhelmed with crime in Montreal in general, and here I was, piling two more cases on them because I'd been attacked twice in about two hours.

I couldn't ask them to take a third case when the woman wouldn't admit to any wrongdoing. I had to stick to what I knew, which was that I had one homicidal patient still in the same emergency bay as me, and two men trying to drag me away outside. Normally, I'd walk home after a shift, but this time, I didn't dare.

How was I going to get home if Dr. Dupuis kicked me out? Tucker was searching for Ryan, and I didn't want to pay for a cab.

I decided to ignore the problem. If I had to, I'd sleep upstairs in a call room until Tucker or Tori could escort me home.

It meant that I was leaving Alyssa without any police support, but if I could convince her to tell them herself, or call the station, that would be even better.

Maybe she'd found Patrick in the meantime. I should check on her, if Dr. Dupuis didn't lock me in the resident's room.

12

"Poor judgment and insight," Dr. Dupuis greeted me when I emerged from the conference room. He'd been waiting for me in the little hall so we could have a semi-private conversation, unless one of the nurses tried to squeeze past us into the kitchen for more coffee.

"What?" I recognized his words as part of the psych evaluation, which was not only figuring out exactly how depressed or anxious patients were. My psychiatry rotation also taught me to check judgment, which was their ability to problem-solve in real life, and their insight, which meant how much they understood their own condition.

"You mean me?" I added, a beat too late.

Dr. Dupuis snorted. "Of course I mean you."

He didn't even give me *impaired* judgment and insight. He said *poor*. Doesn't get any lower than that.

Running into a busy road without looking was poor judgment; poor insight was proclaiming yourself Jesus 2.0 who could jump to the moon and heal minds with maple water and cayenne pepper.

In my head, I started swearing in Farsi. Tucker taught me a few filthy ones. I had no idea how accurate they were, since he got them off his buddies, but I imagined pissing on someone's head until it foamed.

Not that I would actually do that. I needed a reference letter from God in order to battle my way into the Chihuahua-eat-Newfoundlander emergency fellowship program.

"Shape up," said Dr. Dupuis. "When I tell you to stay in and rest, it doesn't mean sneaking into the parking lot."

"Understood." My throat ached as I struggled to sound commanding. I had to spin my tenacity into a better light. Right now, Dr. Dupuis saw me as a loser who'd been attacked by a patient in the ER, then nearly carted off by two men in a parking lot because she'd been too foolish to stay inside, as instructed. Time for Spin City.

"Except I need to speak to Dr. Chia first. Is she still here?"

"Why?" His eyes sharpened and shoulders tensed.

"I'm wearing her white coat. I need to tell her that the men might have been trying to kidnap her, not me. Maybe they saw this." I pointed to the embroidered pocket.

His own lab coat flapped behind him as he strode past the nursing station toward the ambulatory side. "Val. Val!"

She'd already donned her boots and Canada Goose parka, and was tying down the ear flaps on her hat, but when she spied Dr. Dupuis racing at her, she startled, bumping her hip into the ambulatory side counter. "What is it, Dave?"

"You can't go out there by yourself."

She blinked up at him. "What are you talking about? I'm going home. I finally finished my charts."

"No." He advanced on her, almost backing her into the counter.

I would never stand that close to any colleague except Tucker, and I wouldn't do it in public.

"What do you mean, no?" She ducked her head, cheeks flushed. Then she glanced over his shoulder and focused on me. "You okay, Hope?"

I nodded and handed her the white coat, pointing at the embroidered name on the front pocket. "Only I was wearing your lab coat when I was attacked. They might have thought I was you. You should have someone escort you to the parking lot."

She frowned, forming a V in her otherwise lineless face. Even now, I couldn't help admiring her excellent genes in Asian solidarity. "Why would anyone want to attack me?"

Dr. Dupuis raised his eyebrows and rubbed his thumb and forefingers together to symbolize cash.

"Oh, because of the—well, it's Mark's, anyway. It has nothing to do with me."

What did she mean? He was her partner. Unless they kept completely separate finances?

Her cheeks coloured as Dr. Dupuis surveyed her, their noses barely six inches apart. She could probably feel his breath fluttering her bangs. She locked eyes with him, even though she was purportedly talking to me. "I mean, thanks, Hope. I'll see if someone will walk out with me."

"I'll do it." Dr. Dupuis backed up, but she was still mostly sandwiched between him and the desk.

"No! You're the night doctor. You stay here. I'll check in the back, see if Dr. Callendar's finishing up at the same time."

No one answered her. I wouldn't trust Dr. Callendar to protect Henry, my wooden art doll currently arranged in sleeping position beside my apartment laptop.

"I'll find you someone," said Dr. Dupuis.

"Dave, *I can do that.*"

"Val." His eyes burned into hers. He seemed to have grown another foot in height and another in width, looming over her like a grizzly on its hind legs.

Five minutes ago, he'd been intoning, *Poor judgment and insight.*

Not exactly the vibe he was giving off right now.

She glared back at him before she took a step to her right, skirting both him and the desk. "You have a point. Both of you. But it's not your job description to escort me to the parking lot. I can get the security guard, Charles. Or Patrick! Everyone loves Patrick. Julie was singing his praises the other day. Patrick is perfect." She folded the white coat over her arm, ready to go.

The masseter muscle flexed in Dr. Dupuis's jaw.

I piped up, "I can't find Patrick. I was looking for him earlier. He's actually dating the woman in room 13, who looks like she was beaten. I asked him to leave for the rectal exam and the one-on-one history, and he disappeared before he could give me more of a history. Hasn't even texted his girlfriend since 12:30."

Dr. Chia raised her eyebrows. "That's strange. They seemed very close."

"You saw them tonight?"

"No, on Thursday. They were dressed up. He wore a suit and everything."

Strange. "He wore a suit and tie to work, instead of his uniform?"

"He said he'd been called in early for a shift and didn't have time to change after a meeting downtown—"

"That's the person you want to take you to the parking lot?" Dr. Dupuis exploded. "Someone who wasn't even dressed for work two days ago? At least take Charles. He's the head of security. And I'll go out with you so you'll be covered on two sides."

Her brow pleated again. "What about your patients?"

He stared at her.

Her cheeks deepened to carmine, but she didn't blink. They watched each other for so long that I shifted my weight from foot to foot, wondering if I should clear my throat.

Without stirring her eyeballs, Dr. Chia said, "I'll figure something out. Hope, start seeing patients."

Dr. Dupuis opened his mouth. Probably the #2 task on his to-do list was to kick me out of the ER instead of letting me resume clinical duties on a night when every passer-by seemed to hanker for my head.

However, since Dr. Chia ranked at #1, he maintained his staring contest with her and told her, "I'm coming with you."

Those two wouldn't notice if an earthquake buried the rest of us.

I waved goodbye and skipped back to the acute side. Dr. Dupuis would blank out my fuck-ups as he immersed himself in Dr. Chia. Hooray!

Strange that no one had told me about the two of them. Seriously. Not one word.

Tucker's a 24 hour news ticker, fountaining gossip about virtual strangers. I'd overheard references to Dr. Chia's boyfriend Mark, and even the fact that they were trying to have a baby (sorry, there are no secrets in the emerg), and 1.1 million dollars was boiling hot tea, but I was more intrigued by the whole Dr. Dupuis thing.

Dr. Dupuis had never displayed so much emotion in the ER before. He behaved like a robot most of the time. A brilliant, unflappable robot that I liked more than most humans, but a robot nonetheless.

Tonight he and Dr. Chia acted more like me and my men.

Now I understood why the other residents seemed fascinated—and repelled—by me and Tucker and Ryan. Whether or not you approved of a love triangle, when most of the world marched along in ye olde Noah's Ark model, a threesome caught your eye.

I twisted around to check on them. Dr. Dupuis leaned close to her, whispering something I couldn't hear or even lip read.

Her cheeks remained flushed, but she didn't draw away.

She didn't *want* to get away.

And she claimed that Mark's 1.1 million dollars had nothing to do with her.

Only one thing made sense to me. A million dollars wasn't enough to keep Dr. Chia with Mark. She and Dr. Dupuis were either on the cusp or had already hooked up underground.

I picked up the first chart, COUGH, still smiling. I shouldn't pick sides in this. I'd never met Mark. Cheating is wrong. But I liked Dr. Dupuis, and Dr. Chia seemed cool. Maybe they'd be happy together.

"Fuck you! Fuck your twat until it rips up your ass!"

Lori Goody's voice rang down the hall, describing the equivalent of a fourth degree vaginal tear to the boys in blue as they dragged her out of room 14 in handcuffs and ankle cuffs.

I angled my head away from her, trying not to attract her ire en route.

"You can't do this! I know people! Powerful people! People who know things!"

She dragged her feet on the ground. Whatever they'd given her had worn off and left her spitting mad.

I glanced around the ER for someone to take charge. Andrea, Amber, and the préposée, Julie, had gathered around the police in a loose, sober-faced circle. Who'd prescribe the benzos?

Wait a minute. Dr. Callendar had probably taken off as soon as he'd browbeaten the Glen into accepting Lori Goody. Dr. Chia and Dr. Dupuis had disappeared into the parking lot, probably flanked by the chief of security.

That meant *I* was in charge of Lori Goody now.

Actually, I was in charge of the entire emergency department.

Wow.

The white walls and white floors and fluorescent lights spun for a second while I absorbed that responsibility.

Forget great power. I carried Way. Too. Much. Responsibility.

Roxanne appeared at my left elbow, unimpressed with my morphing into Superwoman. "What do you want to give her?"

"What did she already get?" Lori Goody needed all the drugs.

"Haldol 12, Ativan 5, Benadryl 50. She was asleep before they started walking her out. You can't knock her out completely, or she's not safe in a cell, but she can't be like this, either."

Uh oh. I've never had to give multiple doses of Haldol and Ativan. At the most, two doses should do it. My usual dose is 5 mg of Haldol and 2 mg of Ativan, so she'd already more than doubled it, plus the Benadryl, which I found a bit puzzling. Were they using it as an antihistamine?

I brought up my notes for "The Art of the Chemical Takedown," the EM:RAP podcast's two episodes on the best way to sedate a patient.

Ketamine. *No, she can't be so knocked out that she stops breathing in a police car.*

Midazolam. *Okay, well, it's in the same family as Ativan, and can be given IM, plus there's a reversal agent if we need it.* There was still a risk that she might get too sedated, but I'd take the risk with Lori Goody. Elephant tranquilizers seemed more her speed.

One expert did suggest Benadryl in a "B-52," but I'd never seen anyone using it. And anyway, it had worn off in less than four hours.

"Midazolam, 2 mg IV," I said. It was a slightly conservative dose that shouldn't do her any harm and would keep her calm. For cocaine patients, and many others, we keep pushing benzos, benzos, benzos.

"We took out her IV because she was calm before the police started walking her out," said Roxanne.

Right. Lori Goody couldn't keep an IV on the outside in case she ran away from the police and started shooting up on the street with a handy-dandy sterile site.

I double-checked my notes. "Okay, draw up 5 mg of Midaz IM and give 2.5 and 2.5. That should do it without overdoing it."

"Can you write it while I'm getting it?" Roxanne called over her shoulder as she rushed to the med cart in resus.

"Sure," I said, even though I had no idea how to titrate a dose on the computer. So much for making sure a human understood it; you had to make SARKET obey.

The order screen took so long to load, I tried a different menu. No dice.

Maybe the system itself was borked. Certainly Dr. Chia had struggled with SARKET, and I was no expert in the new EMR system. Tucker and I got a day of "super training" before we were thrown in with it. "You're young, you'll figure it out," our trainer told us. "You should see some of the old guys."

That wasn't especially helpful, although Tucker told him the system was "cool."

Tucker thought everything new and different was cool. He was a human personification of ADHD: very hyper, minimal attention. I sometimes worried that his interest in me would flag now that he was no longer fighting over me with Ryan.

I breathed in. And out.

If Tucker did fall out of love with me (and who could blame him?), there was nothing I could do about it.

In the meantime, I finally managed to enter Midazolam with a custom comment to give it in 2.5 mg doses. There.

I grabbed the COUGH chart and popped into the hall between the nursing station and the ambulatory zone to see the elderly smoker with a temperature of 38.2 and a sat of 94 percent. She wasn't wheezing, but her lungs were tight, so I ordered Ventolin and Atrovent and Prednisone and an Xray.

I decided to wait for her film and see how she responded before I gave her antibiotics or stepped up to IV steroids. Tucker was using ultrasound to try and detect pneumonia independent of X-rays, but I didn't feel as confident wielding the ultrasound wand, and I wanted to move onto the next chart. Our wait time had ballooned to 12 hours again, even with Dr. Dupuis practically cloning himself so he could see more patients simultaneously.

Speaking of which, where was Dr. Dupuis? It was cool to run the ER for a few minutes, but after that, I wanted God in the wings.

I trotted through the ambulatory and acute sides, glancing into each room.

No Dr. Dupuis.

No Dr. Chia.

No guard.

A terrible feeling crept along my shoulder blades. *They shouldn't have gone to the parking lot.*

Two men tried to kill me in the parking lot.

Now, I'm a paranoid kind of gal ever since 14/11. Guns to the head will do that to you. If someone got me a cake and a stripper burst out of it, I'd fall on the floor screaming before I cheered his or her G-string.

Something else nagged at me. I'd read a Statistics Canada report on family violence. Murder-suicides are uncommon in Canada, but 95 percent of them are committed by males, and most of them killed their current or former spouses, including common law spouses.

Tonight, two men grabbed me in the parking lot when I was wearing Dr. Chia's lab coat.

And if I read the vibes correctly, Dr. Chia had or would soon have an ex-common law spouse.

I'd thought it was cute that Dr. Chia and Dr. Dupuis were hooking up. But what if Mark the millionaire didn't find it so charming?

The most dangerous time for a woman is when she's leaving her partner. The beloved Toronto family doctor Dr. Elana Fric was killed by her husband two days after she served him with divorce papers.

And I'd let Dr. Chia step out into the night immediately after I'd been attacked.

I approached the middle aged secretary with the punk pixie cut. "Could you page Dr. Dupuis?"

She straightened the cuffs on her white coat. "Don't you have his cell number?"

"No—"

My phone rang.

I didn't recognize the 613 number on my screen.

My heart stilled. That was the area code for Ottawa.

Ryan.

No. It wasn't Ryan's number, which I had memorized.

Nor was it Tucker's 514 number.

Maybe Tucker had picked up a new phone in Ottawa. But why? And how would he manage to do that after 2 a.m.?

"Yes. Hello," I said.

"This is the Ottawa Police, returning your call. Is this Hope, ah, Zee?"

I tried to shift from hyperventilating to slow, calm breaths. "Yes. Hope Sze. You have information about Ryan Wu? Is he okay?"

"I'm calling to gather more information. My name is Gordon McLaughlin. How do you pronounce yours again?"

"You can pronounce it like the letter C."

I heard his chair creak. "Great. Sure. Dr. C. Aren't you the one who found a dead body outside the stem cell lab—"

"Yes, yes." I tried to cut him off.

"—and ran a code on him? With your dog?"

Oh. Maybe he'd even worked on that case, and it was good he'd remembered it. "Exactly. I was with Ryan Wu at the time. It was his foster dog, Roxy. And it's Ryan who's gone missing today."

"Missing, huh?"

"Yes. His parents can't find him."

"Aren't you the detective doctor?" He laughed a bit to himself.

I pretended to laugh too. "Well, you're the real detective. That's why I'm calling you." My friend Ginger told me I'm too blunt. *You've got to learn to stroke them, Hope. Not that way,* she added, at my scandalized look. *Just be...friendly, all right? Smile at them. Flatter them a little.*

WTF. I was never good at that, even before I got PTSD.

How did you learn that on peds? I'd asked Ginger, who was in pediatric residency.

You have to handle the parents.

Time for me to handle the police. Even if I sucked at stroking strangers, I'd do it for Ryan.

I'd do anything for Ryan.

I love you I love you I love you.

"Why are you calling me from Montreal?" said Officer McLaughlin.

"His parents called. I didn't know if they'd called you."

"When was the last time you saw him?"

My heart dropped. "Ah...two weeks ago."

"You think he disappeared two weeks ago?" His voice sharpened.

I started swearing in my head. In English. Which made it riskier that I'd let a swear slip. "No, I want you to talk to his parents. They're the ones who saw him more recently, so...I have his mom's phone number. Cheryl Wu." I rattled off the number.

He marked it down. "When was the last time they saw him?"

"She called me today because she couldn't find him."

"Yes, but when was the last time she saw him? Or anyone saw him."

More internal cursing. "I, ah, don't have the exact time, so if you could contact Cheryl and Rick Wu, they'll be able to give you more details."

Well, of course a cop wouldn't let you skate by like that. By the time I finished talking to Gordon McLaughlin, he knew that Ryan was my ex, I'd had zero in-person or virtual contact for two weeks, and all I had was his mother's phone call to get me all riled up.

"This isn't a lot of information, Dr. Sze," he said.

Gnashing of teeth. "I know. I'm sorry to bother you. I know how it sounds."

"The Ottawa Police Department is very busy, you know."

"I'm sorry. I remember how helpful you were when we found the body, and I don't want anything to happen to Ryan Wu." I decided to be as honest as possible. Stroking be damned in the middle of the night. "I can't talk to him any more because he's blocked me. I know it sounds weird, but I'd never forgive myself if something happened to him because of me. I've made so many enemies."

"That you have." I heard his chair creak. "Okay, Dr. Sze."

"Okay?" The hairs on my neck rose. I hardly dared hope, even though it's literally my name.

"I'll look into it. I can't promise anything, though."

"That's all I want! Thank you, Dr. McLaugh—I mean, Officer McLaughlin!"

He laughed. "Call me Gordon."

When he hung up, I hurried toward the next case, CHEST PAIN in room 3. The electrocardiogram was normal, and the patient seemed to be a sleeping roll of blankets—in other words, no sign of agony. I touched him lightly on the shoulder. "Monsieur Elmi."

He rolled on his back and gave an extra-loud snore.

"Monsieur Elmi. Jacob."

The overhead pager blared, "CODE BLUE, PARKING LOT. *CODE BLEU, STATIONNEMENT.*"

13

What?

"Sorry, I have to go," I snapped at Jacob Elmi, who snorted in his sleep but otherwise seemed unimpressed as I dashed to the residents' room for my jacket.

I'd never done a code in a parking lot before. Part of me cringed at the idea of risking my kidnappers again so soon. Two bodysnatchers could nab me during code chaos, and no one would glance up from the cardiac monitor.

Could those two men have attacked Dr. Chia, Dr. Dupuis, and Charles on their way to her car?

If so, they hadn't only been grabbed like me. They must have been shot or stabbed, because a Code Blue means your lungs and/or heart have stopped working.

What if more than one of the St. Joe's trio had collapsed?

This could be three victims at once—or more, if bystanders had been caught in the crossfire.

I wouldn't head out completely helpless. As I sprinted toward the resus/eye room hallway, I armed myself with a scalpel in my right pocket and, in the left, an 18 gauge, 1.5 inch needle, capped but mounted on a syringe.

I'd have to unwrap them, so they weren't ready-to-go weapons, but better than nothing. Lori Goody had taught me that.

Ten feet ahead of me, Roxanne pushed the steel crash cart, laden with medications and a portable yellow cardiac monitor, in front of patient reg. She was easy to spot in her neon blue parka and nearly-matching gloves.

I ran ahead of her, hand already extended to help her drag the cart over the extra mats that had been put down to absorb the snow and ice and mud in the hallway. "Can you believe this? Did you hear what the case is? Or how many people?"

She seemed to veer the cart away from my fingers, catching my attention even before she said, "You can't come, Hope."

"What are you talking about? A Code Blue? That's my jam!"

Why else had I volunteered to stay up all night, unless I got all the cool cases? I was the solo emergency resident on call. Unlike the daytime, when the hospital teemed with staff, every code here belonged to me.

"Not this one." Roxanne jerked her head back toward the ER doors, signalling me to leave. "You've got to keep running the department. Dave and Val are out there. He told everyone to make you stay in."

I ignored that. "Dave and Val are giving orders? So it's not them? Is it Charles Packard, the security guard? Or someone else, like a patient who collapsed after driving in with a heart attack?" You always heard about those cases, but I'd never done one.

Her stride hitched. She didn't meet my eyes. "It's asystole. That's all I know."

No heart beat, no electrical activity. The worst prognosis, but an incomplete diagnosis, and she hadn't answered who it was. "A new patient, or—?"

"It's not safe for you, Hope. Stay in. That's an order, and you're slowing me down." She shoved the cart over a mat for emphasis. Less than two metres, and she'd be out of here.

My eyes narrowed. I paused before the double doors, blockading her and the crash cart.

Roxanne and I had always been friends, but now she ordered me around like a Shih Tzu.

She was the same size as me, pretty much, and impeded by the crash cart. Would she really call a Code White on me, containing me in here?

I glanced at the empty security guard booth to my left. Dr. Chia and Dr. Dupuis had picked up Charles Packard on their way out, and we hadn't located Patrick.

Which meant that Roxanne had no guards here to back her up in a Code White. Julie, the overnight preposée, was petite as well.

In other words—and I couldn't believe I was thinking this about my favourite nurse—*I could take her.*

Roxanne's brown eyes flashed. She said nothing, but her thin arms tensed as if she envisioned using the crash cart to ram me into the glass doors.

Of course, the glass doors would open as soon as I stepped onto the rubber mat. I could outrun her crash cart and deal with the consequences later. My quads tensed in anticipation.

"Hope. Stay here with your patients. Dr. Dupuis and Dr. Chia have got this."

True. Two fully-licensed MD's already ran the parking lot code as we spoke. Meanwhile, someone else could arrest in the ER while I rushed out into the snow, into the kidnappers' arms.

But this was a Code *Blue!* Also known as #lifegoals.

Roxanne glowered at me. Her arms flexed again.

She and Dr. Dupuis and Dr. Chia were telling me no. Three people I liked and respected.

Roxanne was part of my tribe of "small, fierce women," as author Charles de Lint put it. I didn't want to fight with her.

And she was right. I was slowing her down.

That's the ER's biggest no-no. Don't get in the way. You're putting a life at risk.

If nothing else, I've figured out that my PTSD, post-14/11 judgment is...impaired.

It pissed me off that they were blocking me on this, but if three people I respected were telling me to fuck off...

I moved out of the way.

"Thanks," she tossed over her shoulder as the exit door parted for her crash cart.

I didn't answer as I strode back through the doors to the resus hallway. What could I say?

You're welcome. It's my pleasure to skip out on a code for the first time in my life. Let's do it again soon, okay?

I closed my eyes and took deeeeeep breaths, my fists still clenched, my hair on points.

How was I supposed to learn like this? I'd be running codes solo soon. I needed every bit of experience I could wring out of this horrendous night shift.

I tried to remind myself—*in-hale. Ex-hale*—that, thanks to my shocking call karma and multiple murder cases, I had more medical experience than a set of triplets ten years out of residency. Whatever my life complaints were, they didn't include "I'm always deprived of the most insane cases."

I scooped up the CHEST PAIN chart and rolled my WOW toward stretcher 3. Monsieur Elmi woke up, grey hair askew, dark hands waving through the air, to tell me about his sharp chest pain, "like an electric shock!"

In other words, atypical pain, but he said he'd had an abnormal stress test a few months ago, at a hospital I'd never heard of. Guaranteed that it would take eons for that mini-hospital to respond to a chart request at night. In the meantime, I gave him aspirin, prn nitro, a chest X-ray, and serial troponins, etc. Next.

I had to don a gown and gloves for DIARRHEA. At least it wasn't bloody. Yay.

The next one seemed straightforward, SORE THROAT, but the woman described a headache "like a spider squeezing my head" and numbness in both legs, complaints bizarre enough for me to hold her for Dr. Dupuis.

Good thing I'd spent most of my life in school for this thrilling learning experience. Right on par with a Code Blue.

I kept an eye on the hallway, waiting for any news, any footstep alerting me to the code team's return. Every passing minute, I wanted to dart out to the parking lot. I didn't even know what the case was, or how many people had been affected. I knew only one thing:

Asystole.

No heartbeat. No breathing. So they must have intubated the patient and tried epinephrine. What else?

I tried to smile at the punk rock secretary, who sat at her desk, facing the Plexiglass barrier, as I inquired, "What's going on out there? With the code?"

She pointed to the phone in her right hand and shook her head.

She couldn't talk, she didn't know, or both.

Great. I tried Amber, the nurse bitten by Lori Goody and rewarded with a Clavulin prescription. She gazed back at me, wide-eyed. "It's a young man. That's all I know."

A young man. Usually, that means drugs or trauma, although it could be a pneumothorax or sepsis. Congenital heart disease or arrhythmia, less likely, but still possible.

I picked up a chart for INSOMNIA. Every health care worker on a night shift has deliberate and prolonged insomnia. When I popped into the room, it was empty. The guy had gone home already. I wanted to scream.

The only good news was that our wait time had shrunk to five hours.

Then I heard footsteps in the resus hallway. My head snapped up.

Dr. Chia clipped toward the nursing station, seemingly unbloodied and unharmed, but she met my eyes and shook her head.

Uh oh. My stomach plunged.

Roxanne bustled toward the ambulatory side, giving an almost imperceptible nod in my direction before we both turned away. I found it painful to even look at her. She'd been my friend from nearly the first moment I landed in Montreal, and now it felt like we played on opposite teams.

This time Andrea, my other favourite nurse, navigated the resus cart back into place in the resus room.

Dr. Dupuis brought up the rear, expressionless as usual.

No patient.

Empty hands.

No smiles.

I hurried into resus to buttonhole Andrea, who gave off a comfortable mom vibe and had taken care of me after my first murder case. Even more importantly, she hadn't told me off. I couldn't pretend all was hunky dory with Dr. Dupuis or Roxanne, and Dr. Chia would attract Dr. Dupuis the way I attracted mosquitoes in May.

"Was it Patrick?" I said. Past tense. They hadn't brought him in for blood work and an emergency thoracotomy, so past tense seemed appropriate.

She nodded.

I closed my eyes and tried another few unspoken Farsi swears. It didn't help. "What happened to him?"

"He...was shot in the throat." She busied herself with the IV pumps.

14

—————

Patrick, the gentle, kind security guard, the good boyfriend—someone shot him in the throat?

My body jerked. This was not a trauma hospital. And Montreal was not a violent city in general. The last time someone got shot at this hospital was...14/11.

Even though I'd become somewhat inured to evil, I was shocked into silence tonight. *This didn't happen in Canada.*

Oh, yes, it did.

Andrea nodded at me in solidarity.

I wanted to touch her shoulder, to tell her it was okay, but that would be a lie. Plus we don't generally touch each other, so it would feel awkward, even invasive.

I pressed a hand to my own throat, as if to shield it from any more stray bullets. My weary brain offered, *That gives a whole new meaning to the complaint SORE THROAT*, before I dragged it back on track. "Were you able to do anything—"

"They took him to UCH." University College Hospital, nicknamed UC or UCH. The anglophone trauma centre. For whatever reason, it's not part of the "superhospital" yet. "Dr. Chia called them while Dave ran the code. We were trying to stabilize Patrick until the paramedics got in. He was an obvious trauma."

Yeah. Doesn't get more obvious than *shot in the throat.* Unbidden, my mind played the opening chords to Bon Jovi's "You Give Love a Bad Name," even though they'd sung about a heart shot, not throat. My drowsy brain enjoyed making jokes like a drunken 45-year-old. I forced more relevant words out of my mouth "So he had a heart beat?"

"We were doing CPR. Fluids. Dave intubated him. We didn't have time to give blood—Kris ran to the blood bank and barely grabbed the units in time to hand to the paramedics en route."

In other words, they secured his airway and breathing, reduced the bleeding, and gave him a heart beat through CPR. With any luck, the blood would maintain his circulation long enough to get him to the trauma team.

Still, asystole from a penetrating trauma. Poor prognosis, although not as bad as blunt trauma.

"I was pushing on his wound—" Her voice broke.

This time, I did place my hand on her arm, so softly that I barely touched the hairs, let alone the skin. Still, she closed her eyes and nodded in acknowledgement.

It was the first time I'd seen Andrea crack. ER nurses are tough.

Sure enough, she patted my hand and drew away to rearrange a syringe on top of the trauma cart, which gave me the space to say, "Where was the wound? Front, back, side?"

She pointed to the right side of her own throat. Not the midline, so the shot had likely missed the trachea, but would easily transect the carotid artery or jugular vein, and likely had, since his heart had stopped.

But Andrea had applied pressure to keep whatever blood he had circulating, and Dave had secured his airway, and someone had done CPR while Kris ran for blood and Dr. Chia assembled the trauma team.

I could have done more. I could have wrestled an ultrasound machine outside to check on the vessels, or inserted a central line, or gotten UCH on the horn to liberate Dr. Chia for more advanced work. Probably Dr. Dupuis would still have intubated, because he's God, but I would have helped, damn it, if they'd let me.

"Did you get ROSC?" Return of Spontaneous Circulation.

"We got electrical activity. Dr. Chia thought she felt a pulse at the end, after a bit of fluid, but we didn't want to stop CPR."

Patrick was mostly dead, to quote *The Princess Bride*, but we had to cling to the fact that it meant he was also barely alive. One upside: temperature well below freezing. Hypothermia would slow down his circulation and therefore his blood loss. But he could have easily bled out, depending how long he lay there.

"Any idea when this happened?" I asked.

Andrea shook her head. The colour had returned to her plump cheeks, and she reset the IV pump. "The police are coming to talk to all of us. They'll probably question you, too. You talked to him in room 13, right?"

I closed my eyes. *Yes, I talked to him before I asked him to leave the room. And he got shot.* I couldn't help feeling guilty, although chances were, even if I hadn't given him the boot, he would have had to return to work. Security isn't a no-risk job. "Has anyone talked to Alyssa, his girlfriend in room 13?"

She pressed her lips together and smoothed her patterned pink and blue scrubs over her midsection. "I don't know. You'd better ask around before you go in."

I couldn't rip open her curtain and start blaring away that Patrick had been shot in the throat. But I couldn't let her lie there Not Knowing, either. That was hell, too.

I should leave the decision to Dr. Dupuis and Dr. Chia, Patrick's attending physicians. I'd never treated him. Lack of judgment and insight once again.

My neck twinged. Then I rubbed my eye before I caught myself. I tried not to touch my face when I worked, for fear of giving myself conjunctivitis, vomiting, and diarrhea from the crusty eyes and gastros I waded through every shift. That reminded me of Tucker, which made me tachycardic again. Still. "I will. Thanks for...working on him."

She looked away, steeling her emotions before she spoke again. "He was so nice, even in the middle of the night. And so handsome when he showed up in a suit the other day! I told him his mother would be proud, and he laughed and shook his head."

That was such a mom thing to say. A lump grew in my aching throat. I forced some words past it. "I bet. I wish I could've done something for him besides see patients with diarrhea."

The frown lines on her forehead cleared for a second as a tiny smile touched the corner of her mouth. "Oh, knowing you, you'll do something, all right." She brushed my arm to cheer me up as she maneuvered the IV pole past me. "'They also serve who only stand and wait,'" she tossed over her shoulder.

I grimaced. I knew it was a line of poetry, and why she was quoting it. She was telling me it was okay that I hadn't tended to Patrick at the end. Me running the ER as best I could while they resuscitated him was also a service to him, and to the rest of the team.

But my heart throbbed. My throat burned. My dry eyes smarted. And most of all, fury roiled in my chest and made me clench my jaw.

I stomped out of resus to confront Dr. Dupuis.

On my first day at St. Joe's, he'd called me in for a Code Blue that turned out to be a murder. We'd worked side by side then. What was so different now, that he'd forbid me from joining the code?

First I had to review the patients with him, so I collected my work station and pushed it toward him, which made me feel like an over-burdened camel.

He and Dr. Chia murmured together at the ambulatory desk. Her eyes widened, but he stood up right away, blocking my view of her and swiping his hair away from his eyes. "Thanks for staying in, Hope."

"Why?" I said. One word, but he knew I was simmering with distrust. I was really saying, *Why did you make me.*

He held up his palms as if to ward off the WOW if I tried to kneecap him with it. "I know you're angry."

"Residency is supposed to be about learning. That's why McGill charges tuition and we get paid bupkes. But you blocked me from learning at a code, even though I want to be an emergency doctor. Why?"

Dr. Chia wrapped her white coat tighter around herself before she got up from the desk and walked around us, toward the acute zone, leaving us alone to fight.

"Because I wanted to protect you," he said.

"From what? Because I have PTSD? You were one of the people who gave me a reference letter to come back! Which was—thank you," I muttered. I'm Canadian, polite even in the midst of an argument. I've never shouted at a staff doctor before, let alone my absolute favourite one, and the one I counted on for a reference. My cheeks flared as I fought to reign it in.

"You're welcome," he replied evenly. "No, that's not it. I knew you'd handle it. Any code could traumatize you more, but I knew you wanted to learn and would go nuts if you sat at home for months." He pushed his glasses up and frowned at me, showing the wrinkles around his eyes. "It was for your safety. If the code had been inside, I would have brought you right in. But it was in the parking lot where two men had attacked you. It was a crime scene. What if you'd come out for the code and gotten attacked again? Then we'd have two victims instead of one."

My hands flew to the scalpel and needles I'd stuffed in my pockets. I forced myself to interlace my hands and place them at my navel. A counsellor had given me feedback about how to make my body language less "frantic" and after I'd gotten over feeling offended, I'd started applying her tips at work. "That's my decision. I get to decide my own risks."

Dr. Dupuis didn't blink. "No. As your supervising physician, I make the call. I'll review the case with you, I'll teach you as much as I can, but I couldn't put you at risk for the third time tonight. Sorry."

I exhaled. He wouldn't budge. Even if I continued to object, or brought it up with the residency director, he would stand by his decision. I respected that, even though a tiny part of me still wanted to face punch him.

"It's a marathon, not a sprint, Hope." Dr. Dupuis's nostrils flared. "You'll have tons of codes. With our call karma, we could have another ten tonight. Not worth going out there where we can't protect you."

"You weren't protected, either," I said.

"I was watching everyone."

That was an extra stress for him, literally trying to watch everyone's backs while running a trauma code. I paused to consider that. You think it's hard to pat your head and rub your belly at the same time? Try saving someone's life and watching for stray bullets at the same time.

I tried to reduce my heart rate by concentrating on the facts. "What time did you find him?"

"Val said it was 2:32 a.m."

"How long do you think he was out there? Did you ask his boss to narrow the window of how long he must've been lying on the ground?"

Dr. Dupuis frowned. "Charles was calling for backup and trying to get the police on scene. He thought we might get shot next. He kept yelling, 'Don't shoot!'" He sighed and shook his head. "The guards are under a lot of stress."

It could have been a throwaway line, but something in his voice caught my attention. "You mean they're stressed out about Patrick getting shot?"

"Yes, but...I mean before that." He swept his hand through his bangs. "They were already under a lot of pressure. That whole OR thing—"

"What, exactly, happened?" I'd obviously missed a lot in my month away.

He glanced at me. "You didn't hear? Someone went up to the OR's and cleaned out all the drugs just before Christmas. Midazolam, Fentanyl, intubation equipment, you name it. They scooped everything up, probably had no idea what anything was, so they took it all.

The hospital started an investigation, and heads are going to roll. Security's going to have to take the hit, even though, for the past two months, they've been filing reports about the OR surveillance cameras not working properly. Plus the OR staff should have locked it all up anyway. Doesn't matter."

Shit rolls downhill, Tucker once pointed out to me. The guards were ranked lower than surgeons, operating room nurses, and probably even cleaning staff. Yep, the guards would take the hit. Just like residents work longer hours than staff, and younger doctors cover oversights by overconfident blowhards like Dr. Callendar, the guards would play scapegoat for the OR theft.

I sighed. "You think that's got anything to do with Patrick getting shot?"

"It would be a stretch," said Dr. Dupuis. "I know that he was working that night. So was I. I saw him patrolling the halls. For what it's worth, he acted normal. The police questioned all of us. I told them I was in the ER, but as far as I could tell, the guards were doing their jobs, same as usual."

I tucked that into the back of my exhausted cortex. I'd have to Google the OR theft. That hadn't hit my radar while I was working in Ottawa, but I ignore the news when I'm neck-deep in work. Which is always. Tucker had been in Los Angeles at Christmas, so my gossip hound had missed the action. And our friend Tori prides herself on data instead of dishing dirt, which makes her a saint, but slightly less relatable.

"Okay. I have some other questions about Patrick tonight. I heard his wound was on the right." I pointed an index at my own throat. "You think his carotid and his IJ were hit?"

Dr. Dupuis nodded. "Andrea described what sounded like an expanding hematoma. Nothing pulsatile, but he might not have had enough blood left by the time we came across him."

"How big was the wound?"

Dr. Dupuis held his fingers about a centimetre apart. I didn't know bullets well enough to figure out what kind that would be, but the police would.

"Could you tell the entrance or exit wound?" The exit wound is bigger, because the bullet kind of explodes out of there.

Dr. Dupuis glanced at me sideways, although he understood why I was asking. "We didn't roll him, but the front seemed like the entry site. I palpated a larger exit wound in the back." He held his fingers out about 3.5 centimetres this time.

"So whoever shot him was facing him."

"Looked that way."

Our eyes met straight on. I'd heard of execution-style killings where they shot you from behind. If you couldn't see them, then even if you survived, you couldn't testify against them.

Also, it would take a lot of...detachment to shoot someone from the front.

But why shoot anyone in the neck? Wouldn't you aim for the brainstem if you wanted instant extinction?

To me, a throat shot implied something different. Either you had poor aim, because you'd missed the head entirely—or you had very good aim, and you deliberately zeroed in on the jugular. Or the trachea.

I had to think about this, and we didn't have time to think. We had an increasing tide of patients, and my brain kept firing out useless tidbits.

"Don't dwell on this," said Dr. Dupuis. "It's going to be a long night as it is."

I didn't answer. He should know that I couldn't turn off my brain. Repeatedly telling me no, for my own good, made me want to give him the finger immediately before I cartwheeled off a cliff.

I changed the subject. "Is someone going to tell his girlfriend, Alyssa Taylor, in room 13? She's been trying to reach him for hours."

Dr. Dupuis paused. "We'll have to see who's next of kin. It's probably his parents."

That made sense. You usually don't change your power of attorney until you get married. Still, tears stung my conjunctivae. If something happened to Ryan or Tucker, no one would tell me. I'd have to wait in line. I had to blink and breathe until my eyes dried up again.

"The police and the doctors at UC will contact the next of kin, Hope. They're probably working on him right now."

"I know." I should let Patrick—and my preliminary investigation —fall to the wayside. My job was the patients in front of us, who were legion.

"Let's catch up on the patients you saw."

"Okay." I obediently scooped up the clipboards and tried to load the CHEST PAIN up on my WOW. A little hourglass spun, but nothing happened.

"Try on the desktop. Sometimes it's faster," said Dr. Dupuis, rolling his chair sideways to give me more room at the counter.

He was right. We whipped through the three cases and picked up our next charts.

I couldn't resist checking on Alyssa's blood test results, though. Her pregnancy test had come back negative, which made my face twist, even though her battered body and grieving mind didn't need another stress. Her CT head and face were ordered but pending.

Meanwhile, I kept my fingers and toes crossed for Patrick.

I had to text Tucker.

Bullets in the parking lot. Be careful. Don't come until at least 0700. I love you.

He didn't answer. I left a phone message for him too, to be sure.

I texted my parents next, because I knew they'd worry, and I definitely didn't want my family descending on me to make sure I was okay, only to get blown away too.

And then I texted Ryan. Even though I knew it was hopeless. Even though he was blocking me, it broke the rules, and my very existence on this earth was offensive to him.

Thinking of you.

15

Back to work. Mo' patients, mo' problems.

Andrea beckoned me over to the black landline before I had a chance to enter some orders. I picked up the receiver, conscious of my own heart banging in my chest. Was it possible Ryan or Tucker would call me through the hospital—

"I'm sorry—" Roxanne's high voice came through the phone.

My hand clutched the receiver. Roxanne. Nurse frenemy.

My brain kicked in. We didn't have to stop being friends. In fact, she was apologizing. Maybe she was sorry for blocking me from Patrick's code? No, she was still talking.

"—but could I get some Ativan?"

Oh. Roxanne wanted an order. Ativan was a common benzodiazepine, or sedative. "For you?" I tried to joke.

She half-laughed. "I wish! It would knock me out for the rest of this shift."

It probably would, because she was slender enough to make her Italian grandmother weep, and she probably didn't take drugs on the regular. Unlike some. I glanced at room 14 in case Lori Goody had somehow bounced back.

"It's not for room 14," said Roxanne, reading my mind over the phone. "Room 13 was going nuts in the CT. They couldn't do her. She was rolling her head back and forth. I had to run up."

Alyssa Taylor thrashed so much that they couldn't scan her brain. Too much artifact. As with a regular photo, if the subject was moving too much, the CT scanner couldn't capture a good image, which meant..."Someone told her what happened to Patrick?"

"No. At least, I didn't. But she was trying to get up, trying to rip off her collar—"

I was already entering the order on SARKET, which processed it, for once. "Two milligrams IV okay? But start at one."

"Perfect."

Radiology hated if patients went bananas in CT. Then if we oversedated patients, they shook their heads while we gave an antidote or, if that failed, had to intubate them because they'd forgotten how to breathe.

I still wondered if Alyssa had overheard or had intuited how Patrick was doing. Although Andrea and I had spoken on the other side of the ER, in low voices, most staff wouldn't be that circumspect.

First I had to enter my orders and deal with some VIRAL ILLNESS and COUGH, which was exactly as mesmerizing as one could expect.

Next, I tried to talk to Dr. Dupuis, but he was with a patient.

Meanwhile, I picked up a SEIZURE, which sounded like a fun change of pace, but turned out to be a 22-year-old with known epilepsy who hadn't taken his medication for a week, then indulged in a few beers. Nothing for me to do except recommend taking his anti-epileptics, not alcohol, and to draw blood levels for Valproic Acid et al.

When Dr. Dupuis and I convened again, on the ambulatory side, as distant from room 13 as we could get, I pounced on him to whisper about Patrick.

He shook his head. "He didn't make it."

I wanted to scream. I wanted to howl.

No. He was young and healthy.

No. God and Dr. Chia had worked on him.

No. Maybe I could have saved him.

I wrenched my head to the side, like I was the one with the seizure.

"Yeah," he said. "I know."

Then he disappeared with an armload of charts, because we still had to hustle to see the living.

The perfect emergency doctor: one who never dwelled on death.

What did that make me, the murder magnet? I tried to shake that off by picking a happy memory, as one therapist had suggested. I closed my eyes and imagined petting Roxy, Ryan's foster dog. I could sink my fingers into the thick, black fur of her shoulders. She would sit before settling on the ground with a sigh, rolling on her side, paws up to make room for tummy rubs.

Dr. Chia dropped into the chair beside me, looking too tired to move. A male police officer nodded at her sympathetically before collaring Dr. Dupuis into the conference room for questioning.

Dr. Dupuis laid down his stack of charts, and I felt momentarily defeated at the prospect of trying to work my way through them solo after graduation.

"Are you okay?" I asked Dr. Chia. I'd avoided her since my first, dreadful shift with her in July, and I usually wouldn't ask staff any personal questions, but I had to make an exception on the world's worst night shift.

She nodded. Even that seemed to take an effort. "But I'm too tired to drive home."

"You want my call room? I probably won't use it." Even so, I felt a pang. Hard to give up the potential of a quiet room and a bed with clean sheets.

Dr. Chia shook her head. "I can always find a call room upstairs."

"With the plastic-covered pillows," I said, since that was my friend Anu's number one complaint. They covered the pillows to protect them from patient bodily fluids, but every time you turned over, the plastic creaked under your ears and woke you up. Personally, if I ever got to sack out, I was so tired that I blocked out the ear noise, but the springs poking my back or the mattress sagging in a U shape made for a restless few hours.

That won a smile out of Dr. Chia. "Nothing makes for a better night's sleep."

Even in the middle of the night, I admired the shape of her eyes, the point of her chin, and the gloss of her shoulder-length hair. She had a delicate kind of beauty, combined with intelligence and determination. I could see why Dr. Dupuis would chase her. Honestly, if I hadn't messed up our first shift together, I'd like her too. Of course she was four times better-looking than Dr. Dupuis, but beautiful Asian woman/nerdy white guy seemed like a common scenario.

Good thing Tucker was cool, and I never felt model-worthy. My parents always prized brains over beauty.

I scooped up another SORE THROAT chart. When I emerged, Dr. Chia had disappeared, presumably to find a bed upstairs. I labored to enter the throat swab on SARKET, keeping an eye on the conference room door.

The police probably wouldn't interview me, since I never made it out of the ER for Patrick's code, but if they needed me, I'd make myself available. Maybe they'd even drop a few details about the case. Unlikely, but a girl can dream.

Julie, the petite preposée/orderly rushed up to take the swab from me, her eyes so wide that I could see the whites around them. "Can you believe it? Patrick's *dead!*"

I nodded. "Horrible." When there are no words, only the trite ones will do.

"He was such a good guy!"

I nodded. Patrick had seemed very sweet.

"And a badass."

"He was?" I remembered his hands trembling when he had to handcuff Lori Goody. Was Julie rewriting history to make him seem tougher, now that he was dead?

Julie swiped a label out of the blue plastic basket on the table and affixed it to the swab, nodding slowly. "My boyfriend was...you know."

She raised her eyebrows, gave a silent whistle, and glanced at me out of the corner of her eyes.

I nodded, even though I wasn't sure what she meant. Hot? Insane? Both?

She tossed the label backing into the garbage, still talking. "Jesse screamed a lot, except when he was high, but sometimes he was okay. Once he bought a little Transformer toy for my son. You know Bumblebee? The black and yellow one?"

I didn't, but I nodded again. The way she said "my son", it sounded like Jesse wasn't the biological father.

"Yeah. Jason was crazy about Bumblebee. He called it Bumbee. He played with it until it broke, and then he cried. He was only three, you know? He'd pick it up, and it still wouldn't work, and he'd freak out all over again. I told him I'd buy him a new one, but he'd have to wait, because my job doesn't pay much, you know?"

Plus she probably gave her money to the boyfriend, to keep him high instead of hollering. But I murmured, "I know." Working as a preposée doesn't mean raking it in, either. Both things were true. It squeezed my heart that her son had to wait for what sounded like a cheap toy.

"Jesse was pissed off that Jason broke Bumbee and was moping around about it. 'Get over it, you little sh—'" She stopped, cheeks coloured. "I mean, it got on his nerves. Plus I was in a bad mood. It was right before I went on the rag, you know?"

I was forced to nod again, even though I was never particularly "hormonal," and I didn't like the implication that women were incapacitated once a month. Still, in November, I'd come across one of the other female residents, who was normally sharp and strong and decisive, riddled with menstrual cramps on the resident room couch. She really was incapacitated.

"So Jesse was yelling when he drove up to St. Joe's to drop me off in the front circle. That was...I mean, I can handle it. But this time, he kind of—he hit me in the face. Not hard," she added right away. "Just to shut me up. I was shouting at him. It was my fault, you know?"

I stared at her. I'd run out of nods.

"Patrick flew out of the front doors. He made Jesse get out of the car. He told Jesse he wasn't allowed to hit people, and that he could press charges. He said all sorts of stuff. And you know how tall Patrick is—was. Jesse wouldn't look at him the whole time he was talking, but he heard it, and Patrick made him sign a piece of paper that he was trespassing and wouldn't come back on hospital property. He was a *badass*."

Yes, he was. Go, Patrick, go. I had to know more. "So what happened to Jesse? He stopped driving you to work?" He obeyed Patrick?

"Yeah." Julie's face fell. She started playing with the throat swab, rolling it back and forth on the counter. "I had to walk. We didn't have the extra money for bus fare. It took too long, so I couldn't pick Jason up from day care any more, but I signed the papers that Jesse could pick him up too, because he worked nights, so he was home in the daytime. He could get Jason."

My skin prickled. I could hardly breathe. "And did he?"

"Yes, but—" She broke eye contact and started shuffling her feet. "Don't you already know about this? Everyone knows about this."

"I don't. I only came to St. Joe's in July, and I've been away for a research block. No one told me anything."

She tapped the throat swab on the counter, three quick little raps that sounded like the beginning of SOS in Morse code. "It's too hard to say."

"Okay. You don't have to talk about it."

Tears filmed her eyes. "I don't think I can. I didn't mean to—I just wanted to say how great Patrick was."

And she rushed away, barely remembering to deliver the throat swab to Amber, who had walked up to her with her hands open.

16

W hat happened to little Jason?

Four police officers exited the ER, talking amongst themselves. They'd managed to cover Dr. Chia, Dr. Dupuis, both nurses, and maybe even Charles Packard. Although I hadn't gone outside, I heard that the parking lot was also cordoned off for investigation.

I eyeballed these officers' backs, wondering if they already knew about Patrick's conflict with Jesse. I wouldn't accost them before I gathered the whole story—I didn't even know how long ago Patrick had confronted him—but I had trouble concentrating on my next patient's SORE EAR, knowing that Patrick had made at least one enemy at work.

I don't want an incident, Patrick had said when he hesitated to cuff Lori Goody.

Did he mean Jesse? Had something gone wrong after Patrick played the hero? Patrick still had his job, so he hadn't been fired, but he could have been on probation. I should ask Charles Packard.

"I'm allergic to penicillin," said the 40-year-old man with the SORE EAR, who'd yelped when I pulled on his pinna to get a good look at his red right eardrum.

"Of course you are," I said. High dose amoxicillin was first line for otitis media. It worked over 90 percent of the time, and sometimes kids even cheered that they were getting the "banana medicine." Only ten percent of patients who claimed they were allergic to pen turned out to be truly allergic, but between the scads of the supposedly allergic and the parents who asked for "something stronger," I ended up giving a mini-lecture every time I saw a SORE EAR. "What's your reaction?"

"I don't know. I was a baby. My mom told me never to take it." He scratched his head.

I tried to ignore the flakes of dandruff shining on his scalp that might be wafting their way toward me. "Can you take Cefuroxime or other antibiotics called cephalosporins?"

"I don't know. I got a rash with something that sounded like that. Is it on my chart?"

I shook my head. "Only the penicillin." I was not going to probe any further at 3:30 a.m. "We're supposed to allow 48 hours with an ear infection, to see if your own immune system can kill the bacteria. So I'll write you some ear drops for pain in the meantime, and you can start these antibiotics at the 48 hour mark."

His lip jutted forward in a way that made it clear he'd run straight for a 24-hour pharmacy. "The one with a B worked the last time."

I sighed to myself as I entered the prescription for Biaxin. In Halifax, they reviewed the evidence, and then the family and emergency doctors agreed not to give antibiotics to not-very-sick kids and adults before 48 hours. Overprescription promotes antibiotic resistance, which means that antibiotics will stop working, and Scandinavian studies showed that some patients can fight off the ear infections themselves. But in the chaos of Montreal, I resorted to giving a conditional prescription, trying to educate the patients I encountered, still knowing that many would hit the pharmacy before I hit the sheets.

While I printed and signed the ear prescription, I noted that Dr. Dupuis had managed to plow through what seemed like a dozen patients. SARKET labeled our patients as red (me) or him (black), so at a glance, everyone could marvel that he'd buzzed through three patients to every one of mine, even though he'd run a code in the parking lot and I'd started an hour before him.

"Don't worry about it," he said, when he noticed me silently toting up the patient census. "You're here to learn. Plus you were attacked twice. You should go home. Anyone you see is a bonus."

"Thanks," I said, picking up the next chart for KNEE PAIN. "Could I ask you something off-topic?"

He nodded so curtly that I glanced at his feet. Tucker had taught me bit about body language, namely to watch people's lower halves.

They may mouth the correct platitudes, but their feet will point where they're actually thinking. For example, if a woman squeals, "I'm so excited for you! We'll be like sisters!" while her stilettos pivot for the door, brace yourself for a little sibling rivalry.

Dr. Dupuis's feet had turned toward the call rooms. I glanced at the secretary's desk, where the resident room's key still lay on the Plexiglass window ledge. Dr. Chia hadn't taken me up on my bed offer.

Ha. I suspected that instead of heading for the plastic pillows upstairs, Dr. Chia had zonked out in Dr. Dupuis's bed like a very welcome Goldilocks. I smiled to myself. Proof there was life in the midst of carnage.

He wanted to protect Dr. Chia. If only he knew that I'd never ask about his romantic life. Not only would that be hideously embarrassing for all three of us, but I couldn't risk him replying, "How's yours?" I still hadn't heard from Tucker or Ryan.

Still, overall, good news for me. He'd rather talk about anything than Dr. Chia. Which included murder.

"Did Patrick Warren have any enemies?" I asked, straight out.

Dr. Dupuis brought up some lab work to scroll through as we spoke, maybe to avoid my eyes. "Not that I know of."

"Right. That's what I thought, too. But no one's a hundred percent."

He shrugged, closed the window, and opened another. "Is that everything?"

"No." I cleared my throat, which provoked a short coughing fit. So unprofessional. I needed water and throat lozenges and sleep.

He entered some orders as he waited for me to speak.

I nodded my head at Julie, who had disappeared into the stock room. "What happened to her son? You know who I'm talking about?"

"Yeah. Jason." He frowned and made brief eye contact with me.

"What happened to him? And when did it happen?"

Dr. Dupuis shook his head. "Why are you digging this up?"

"Julie told me that her boyfriend, Jesse, hit her in front of the hospital. Patrick was on duty. He ran up and told him off, so she thinks Patrick is—was—a superhero, but got too upset to tell me what happened to her son."

He sighed. "Jesse beat up her son after he picked him up from day care. She had to take him to the Children's."

The Children's Hospital. The beating was severe enough to require medical attention. I sucked in my breath and tried to count at least one blessing: if she took Jason to the Children's, it meant he had survived the beating.

I'd heard of this circle of abuse. The father hit the mother, who hit the oldest kid, who hit the middle kid, who hit the youngest kid, who beat the dog. Once Jesse couldn't beat Julie anymore, he attacked her son.

I focused on the most relevant question. "Where is Jesse now?"

"Last I heard, he was in custody."

"Good." Jesse wasn't a suspect if he was incarcerated, which would turn this into a dead end, but at least he was serving time for beating Jason. Still, I'd have to verify that he was in jail. "When did you last hear about him?"

"Maybe two years ago."

"Two *years* ago," I repeated. That was ages. Jesse could have been sentenced and released already. "What's his last name? Do you know?"

Dr. Dupuis pressed his lips together. "Hope, I know what you're doing."

I nodded. It wasn't like I was trying to hide it. I was trying to find Patrick's killer. Who the hell wouldn't?

"This is not and should not be your priority. First, you need to look after your own health. Next, if you insist on staying, you're here to do your job as a resident."

I felt sick. I always worried about being good enough. Medicine requires every last one of your brain cells and then some. How could I possibly compete when I was always trying to do three things at once?

Dr. Dupuis waved away my expression. "I'm not trying to shame you. I have no issues with your performance. You're still looking after patients and answering questions better than most residents. But you need to look after yourself. Get into shape mentally and physically. When that's over, you can take on the world. Not now."

"Dave." My cheeks got hot, calling him that, but he'd first introduced himself to me as Dave Dupuis, and the nurses first-named him all the time.

He stared back at me, partly startled by my use of his own given name.

"Patrick was shot in our own parking lot. How can I *not* take this on?"

"By delegating it." He looked me straight in the eye. "We did the best we could to save his life, but your job is not to become a vigilante or a homicide investigator. Your job is either to go home and rest, or stay here and work on our living patients. If you keep splitting yourself in different directions, you will be ground to powder within the next six weeks."

Now my face flamed. His words socked me in the gut. Yes, I needed to learn how to delegate. As a med student and resident, my job had been to

a) Drink from the fire hose of knowledge;

b) Suck it up; and

c) When higher-ups asked me to jump, I'd leap into the air faster and more gracefully than anyone else, and do it twenty times in a row, until my competition crumbled.

Except this wasn't sustainable. One of the ortho residents had smiled when I asked about his gruelling half-decade residency program. He said, "It's fine if you accept you won't have a life for five years."

I couldn't smile back, because I'd already forgone a life for eight years of high school plus a summa cum laude university degree, even less of a life for four years of medical school, and now I was enduring up to three more years of worst life in the history of lives.

So once again, God was right. I had to delegate.

And I'd already begun. Tucker searched for Ryan at this very instant, because I was physically tied to St. Joe's tonight. That hurt.

Could I drop Patrick's case? Could I say to myself, *Oh, I've delegated this. The police are handling it. Time to check on bunions.*

Was that what normal people did?

"I hear you," I said finally. "I know you're...wise."

He grinned. "Not really. Just been around the block a few more times."

I managed a minute smile in return, partly because he got unraveled about Dr. Chia. It made him more human than deity.

"So go see some more patients."

Ah. The perpetual punchline. Yet in my brain, I agreed with him. I'd try to delegate. Until 8 a.m., a scant few hours away.

What could happen in less than five hours?

17

I grabbed a chart for FATIGUE, another winner of a complaint in the dead of night. Dr. Dupuis nodded in approval as I rolled my WOW toward exam room number one on the ambu side.

When I raised my fist to knock on the door, I started to cough again. I paused to recover. Following Dr. Dupuis's lead, I used the forced downtime to check on my patients' results.

Alyssa Taylor's CT had come back.

I rolled my WOW to the desk to call UC's trauma team. A male resident answered, sounding harried. "We're stuffed. She can see plastics in the morning. Anything else besides facial trauma?"

"CT head negative. Lots of bruises, including marks on the throat like near-strangling. Her urine is clear. Pregnancy negative. Stable vitals." I listed them all, belatedly.

"If it's only a single system, she should go direct to plastics. Call back after 8 a.m." Plastics was lucky because they got to sleep in. Of course, calling them after 0800 would delay my own departure in the morning, but no one cared about that. He added, "Don't forget the sexual assault team, if needed."

"She denied sexual assault, and most injuries seemed to centre around her head and neck. Hang on. Did you work on Patrick, the gun shot wound to the neck?"

He paused, not hanging up but not giving anything away, either.

"He was the security guard at St. Joe's, and the boyfriend of this patient, Alyssa Taylor. I'm about to go see her." My throat caught again, but I managed to keep going after one hitch. "Is there anything else you can tell me about his case? She doesn't know what's going on."

"Ah...I don't know if I'm supposed to disclose anything to the family. She's not next of kin, right?"

"I don't think so." I cursed myself for taking the wrong lead after they'd already warned me that Alyssa probably wasn't next of kin.

"Yeah. Um, look. It sucks, but I don't think I'm supposed to talk about it. It's a criminal case. The police were here."

"Here, too." I closed my eyes. Going by the book meant shutting me out. Delegating me out.

"Right. So sorry, okay?"

"Okay. Thanks. 'Bye." I hung up. Patient confidentiality 1, Hope zero.

My throat convulsed. More coughing. I darted toward the kitchen/break room to gulp down some water. I couldn't risk imitating pertussis in the middle of my history or physical exam. Someone had brought in a bag of butterscotch candies, so I popped one in my mouth, willing my vocal cords to relax.

The break room placed me in the same corner of the ER as bed number 13, where Alyssa had returned from her CT head. I ought to give her the results of her CT, right? That was part of patient care. She'd want to know about her brain scan.

And about Patrick, if she didn't already know.

I slipped behind her curtain without drawing it open. Ideally, Dr. Dupuis wouldn't detect my shadowy form behind the drape. I left my WOW inside the break room so I could slide in and out faster. The WOW would annoy any nurses who wanted coffee, but I aimed for a quick, covert visit.

"Alyssa," I whispered, as my eyes adjusted to the twilight colour of the room. Although they'd turned off the lights in patient rooms, the nursing station continued to emit a fair amount of wattage. "Ms. Taylor."

I had to suppress another cough, so I rolled the candy in my mouth, urging my body to produce more saliva while I gathered my bearings. The lump of her body didn't stir. Her breathing came deep and even, stuttering occasionally on mucous or blood.

She was still wearing her C-collar, but she'd fallen asleep.

Not exactly surprising around 4 a.m., especially after I'd helped knock her out with Ativan, but still disappointing.

"Hi, Alyssa," I said, more loudly. Although no one wanted to be yelled awake, I couldn't sneak up on a woman who'd been assaulted.

Her bruised eyes stayed closed. Her breathing didn't alter.

I yearned to tap her shoulder or stomp my feet. I could use the excuse that I'd check her neuro vitals, ensuring that her pupils were equal and that she was oriented. But her nurse had already checked them half an hour ago and found them normal. She wasn't due for a neuro check for another 30 minutes.

No, I'd stick to informing her about her CT results.

I whispered now, "Alyssa."

She didn't stir.

"Hey. I wanted to tell you that your CT head is normal, and your neck X-rays look great. So if I examine your neck now and you don't have any more pain, and your neurological exam is normal, I can take off your neck collar, which will make you more comfortable." I touched her hand. "You feel that?"

No response.

"Alyssa?"

She exhaled.

"You have multiple facial fractures. I'm sending you to plastic surgery in the morning. We should sew up your ear."

She gave a faint snore.

I could force her to wake up. I'd pried open patients' eyelids before. But my friend Ginger said that when they rounded at Sick Kids' Hospital, they believed in the healing power of sleep. That meant they only rounded when the patients were awake. So they disrupted their own schedules for the sake of letting the kids get some more shut eye, because they prioritized children's health.

And, in truth, I didn't know exactly how to respond if she asked about Patrick. I could outline the code here and tell her he'd gone to UC. I could say we'd done everything, but it wasn't enough. He hadn't made it.

Except—was it even legal for me to disclose his death? Everyone kept telling me to stay mum.

Delegate.

Leave it to the police.

So I tiptoed out of the room without turning on the light or trying harder to wake her or pry any answers out of her.

Later, I would regret this.

In the meantime, I had to hurry through more patients, pretending to keep pace with God. I rolled my WOW out of the break room before a nurse laid a curse on my firstborn.

As I crossed the ER toward room 1, on the ambulatory side, I scanned for Julie, Jason's mother.

Orderlies did a lot of work, some of it invisible to me as I buzzed from patient to patient. They kept the ER running smoothly, whether they were called health care attendants, personal support workers, or in Montreal, preposés. (They got an extra e, as in préposées, if they were female.)

Préposés performed electrocardiograms. They could apply splints and assist with casting fractures, if they received extra training and the hospital allowed it. They wheeled patients to and from X-ray. They ran blood and urine samples and, yep, throat cultures up to the lab.

During a Code Blue, they often pounded on the chest, doing CPR. During a Code White, they held down the Lori Goodys until we strapped them to the bed for chemical sedation. They stocked the procedure carts to prevent me hunting for the 1.5 inch 25 gauge needle every. Single. Time.

Plus they performed a lot of work that the patients found more healing than the blood tests I ordered: they handed out lunch trays, they helped bathe, they assisted people to and from the bathroom, and they'd fix a diaper.

So as I started my next round of patients, I didn't raise an eyebrow over Julie's disappearance. Maybe she was a "float," moving to different hospital wards overnight, meaning that the ER would only get her occasionally.

However, after I finished FATIGUE and BACK PAIN with no sign of Julie, my throat dried up, and my teeth seemed to ache from the butterscotch.

Where did she go? No break lasted that long, post cutbacks.

Everyone seemed to evaporate tonight.

Ryan had gone AWOL.

Tucker had decamped after him. According to my Finding Friends App, he'd landed somewhere in Ottawa, nowhere near Ryan's apartment or his parents' house. But for whatever reason, Tucker had stopped answering my texts.

Patrick had left the ER and gotten shot in the throat.

I had almost disappeared, if two guys in the parking lot had gotten their way.

It seemed like people kept vanishing tonight. I felt like Roxy, the worried Rottweiler: if I couldn't see them, if they weren't in my immediate radius, I couldn't concentrate on sore ears and bloody bums.

My pack might be in danger. Saint Hope must rush in to save them, barking the entire time!

Who else would vaporize next?

18

"Where's Julie?" I asked Andrea, joining her at the nursing station after I finished reviewing my cases with Dr. Dupuis.

Andrea shook her head, tucking her thick, brown hair behind one ear. "I haven't seen her lately. Roxanne had to run up to the lab herself. We paged Julie, but—"

"How long has she been missing?"

Andrea frowned at me. "I wouldn't say she's *missing*. We haven't seen her recently, and she didn't answer her phone, but you know how the system cuts out. It wasn't urgent enough for us to page her overhead at night. Roxanne didn't mind running up."

We avoided unnecessary paging over the loudspeaker at night because it would rouse the patients, but c'mon, this ain't no ordinary night shift. I said, "She told me that her ex had a run-in with Patrick, and Patrick was shot tonight."

Andrea clapped a hand to her mouth before she caught herself, glancing side to side to check if anyone else had noticed. "You think— you're worried that—"

"I don't know anything for sure. Dr. Dupuis remembered her ex in custody two years ago. Does anyone know if he's still in jail, or if he served his time and got free?"

Andrea shook her head. "No one told me. You think Julie's ex-boyfriend might have been the one...dear God."

No use asking her Jesse's last name, then. Poor Andrea, so innocent. I scanned the ER, wondering who might spill. Not Amber, the new hire fresh out of nursing school. I needed someone who'd signed up for St. Joe's at least two years ago, and who cared about the staff enough to ask about their families. I still wanted to follow up on Jason and make sure that he was okay too.

I'd text Tucker yet again. I might have to resort to Roxanne, but there were other nurses. Linda was the right age, although we'd hardly spoken apart from the "not my first rodeo" debacle. If Dr. Chia woke up, she might help me too.

In the meantime, I turned back to Andrea. "Look. I don't want to worry anyone, but I'm concerned because Julie gave me that information and went poof on the same night that Patrick was killed. If we knew where she was, I could ask her myself. It's a two-fer, making sure that she's okay and checking whether or not her ex is a suspect in shooting Patrick."

Andrea's hands knotted. She forced herself to relax them. "Julie has to be okay."

"Can you help me find her?"

Andrea nodded. "I'm going on break in the next ten minutes. I'll find her." Dr. Dupuis had glanced over his shoulder at the two of us. She said, "You have to get back to work. Leave this with me."

She, too, wanted me to delegate.

I gnashed my teeth for a second, but Tucker had joked about Buffy the Vampire Slayers and her "Scoobies," which meant her investigative team. It also sort of meant her underlings, but anyway. Andrea wanted to take on this piece, and I couldn't press pause on work for more than two minutes without attracting the evil eye.

"I've known Julie for three years. I'll find her," said Andrea. "Go."

I fielded a UTI (yes, a urinary tract infection with frequency, dysuria, and no hematuria, oh my) with Macrobid, one of my personal favourites because it killed 98 percent of E. Coli on the antibiogram. Then I managed a COUGH and an ASTHMA before I snuck in a quick Google.

I couldn't find anything solid on Jesse. They withheld perpetrators' names in child abuse cases in order to protect the children's identity, and unfortunately, beating a three-year-old wasn't a scandalous enough case to create headlines two years later.

Was the guy still in jail or not?

This was when I could use a buddy on the police force, like the private eyes in any good detective novel. Unfortunately, only one, Officer Visser, had seemed friendly, but never so cozy as to pass on her cell phone number. Even if she had, I couldn't risk waking her up to inquire about a child beating two years ago.

I decided to reverse-engineer the problem and take a gander at Patrick instead. What if the good guard had made some headlines himself?

Reader, I Googled him.

A search for Patrick Warren yielded all sorts of false results because it was two first names. Even deliberate quotes around "Patrick Warren" brought up the wrong people, including a famous musician-producer and a truly sad case of a "milk carton kid" who'd disappeared in 1996.

I tried to filter results by geographic area before I gave up and pulled out my phone to check social media. I mostly only used Insta, Messenger, and WhatsApp to communicate with a few friends who'd semi-abandoned their e-mails, but I kept up a nominal social media presence. Patrick and I might have friends of friends in common.

The first thing I noticed was that Patrick had abandoned his personal Twitter account five years ago after Tweeting a few articles on police safety and gun control. He seemed more active on Instagram, where his handle was @policeur.

I frowned. Policeur was a play on police, and he'd used an "eur" ending because it was French-sounding. Patrick had mostly liked #police photos, including pictures of a curvy brunette in uniform, a K-9 staring out of a barred police car window, and a movie-worthy shot of five men in front of an explosion, hashtags #operacoesespe-ciais #bombsquad.

In other words, Patrick idolized police officers.

So why did he join the security guards instead of the police force?

Maybe the guard work was a preamble, padding his résumé before he applied. But when I searched, the path to policehood in Quebec seemed pretty simple: he'd go to CÉGEP, which was a sort of pre-university or technical college for all Quebecers, and choose three years of police technology. Then it was 15 weeks at l'École nationale de police du Québec. He'd pass their exams, apply to a police force, and boom.

One reporter mentioned how few people of colour joined the police: out of 250 new cadets, only 7 described themselves as visible minorities.

"We don't have control over the people who apply," an officer said. Another added that immigrant parents discouraged their kids from joining their force.

I shook my head at these typical Quebec comments: there might be some truth to them, but they never recognized their own instinct to blame the people who didn't apply instead of considering ways to make their program more hospitable.

I glanced at a few more articles about how, at the moment, the police aggressively recruited every race and gender.

Even more reason for @policeur to join their ranks. Surely the income, the job security, and the benefits would galvanize a security guard. I couldn't come up with any good reason to stick to the hospital except that Patrick and Alyssa rented an apartment next door. You could always find another apartment in Montreal.

Who could spill the beans (dark roast!) on Patrick Warren? Charles Packard hadn't seemed chatty, but maybe he'd thaw at end of shift. I'd wake up Alyssa before 8 a.m. And I'd keep inquiring around the ER if God didn't notice. Or maybe, best of all...

Yes! After I handled a VIRAL ILLNESS and another COUGH, I caught sight of two men in uniform, wearing blue shirts and navy pants.

The remaining two guards patrolling the hospital had finally made it to the ER, cutting through the nursing station.

I rushed toward a 20-something blond guy with freckles and longish hair who looked more like he should be playing air guitar than defending the hospital. Well, I hurried as fast as my WOW would allow. If Dr. Dupuis spotted us, I could pretend our convo was medicine-related or start tapping on my keyboard.

"Hey," I said to the guard.

"Hey." His hospital badge named him Michel Raynaud. He glanced at his partner behind him, a fiftyish, six foot tall, stocky white guy who nodded at me, and whose name seemed to be David Miller. I'd glimpsed David guarding the front doors earlier tonight.

"My name is Hope Sze. I'm one of the emergency doctors. So sorry to hear about Patrick."

"Yeah," said Michel. He checked David Miller, who nodded at me, but didn't speak. Clearly a strong, silent type.

I focused on Michel. Of the two, he'd actually spoken to me. A better omen. "Did you see Patrick tonight, before he was...attacked?"

Michel opened his mouth, but David replied first. "We were doing rounds."

"Yes, I heard Patrick was doing rounds too. That's why he was in the parking lot. How many guards are usually working at the same time?"

"We got three right now," said David.

"But normally you'd have four? If Patrick hadn't been—" My cheeks flushed. Everyone told me I was too blunt when I questioned people, but my minimal reserves of tact deserted me in the wee hours of the morning. "I mean, your normal team is four?"

Michel shifted from foot to foot and glanced at Roxanne, who stood at stretcher 6, but whose gaze pierced us through the Plexiglass window. Dr. Dupuis wasn't the only one watching me.

"It's supposed to be the two of you, Patrick, and Charles Packard tonight?" I asked.

At long last, Michel nodded.

Phew. A tiny breakthrough. "Are you calling someone in to replace Patrick?" If so, I had one more potential interview candidate.

"The boss is taking care of it." David laid his hand on the steel baton clipped to his belt.

"The boss" must mean Charles, but my eyes rested on the collapsible baton. I bet it extended as long as a light sabre. Brute force and a longer arc would make it a formidable weapon.

Beside it hung a second weapon. I was surprised that security guards wore tasers as well as batons on their belts. Weren't those for police officers?

"I didn't know you had tasers." I couldn't remember if guards carried tasers at the hospitals in London, Ontario, where I'd gone to medical school. I never used to pay attention to that sort of thing, but ever since 14/11, I'd studied up on guns, ammo, and weapons in general as a forewarned/forearmed mechanism. "Did you always have them?"

David nodded. "For the past two months."

I sucked the breath between my teeth. Two months ago was November. After the hostage taking, St. Joe's had made a big to-do about installing a metal detector at the main entrance and at the ER entrance, as well as increasing the number of security guards. They'd obviously added to the guards' weaponry as well. That was good, but I hated any reference to 14/11 that caught me unawares.

Michel read my expression and glanced uncertainly at David, who waved farewell at me. Michel nodded, and they swivelled toward the doors beside the old light boxes.

"Hang on." I scrambled to pick one last and most important question. "Did you know anyone who had a grudge against Patrick? Who might have wanted to hurt him?"

David shook his head. He reminded me of a bull, mainly because he was large and slow-moving, but dangerous if he was roused. "Gotta get back. We do rounds every hour."

That made sense. I felt comforted at their determination to do their jobs, even though one of their colleagues had fallen in the line of duty. I couldn't hold them up any longer. "Be careful. Were you in the parking lot with Patrick, protecting the staff during the code? Thank you."

"You're welcome," said David, already moving away, Michel in his wake.

I felt a lump in my throat. I wanted to yell after them, *Don't go back to the parking lot! Make sure you wear your coats and bulletproof vests, if you have them! Watch your backs! Literally!*

I sent a silent prayer toward them, even though I'm agnostic. They also serve, who stand and wait and patrol.

They didn't look back.

19

The next patient's KNEE PAIN looked more like plantar fasciitis, but in addition to his heel pain, the guy had slipped on the ice the week before and bumped his knee, so I sent him to X-ray. I also handled a SORE TOE that looked like gout. Dr. Dupuis gave me the thumbs up and kept working.

Since that didn't take too much brainpower, my mind flipped back to Patrick. Four guards on duty made sense to me. One could stay at the main desk, greeting patients, paging doctors overnight, and handing out call room keys. One would guard the ER doors. And two patrolled the rest of the hospital.

Tonight, after Patrick's death, I bet Charles performed double duty indoors, covering the ER entrance and paging people, while David and Michel covered the floors. The main doors were supposed to be locked overnight anyway, although staff ignored this edict when they left around midnight or reported for night shift duty, shouting cheerful hellos to each other.

I checked my watch. If guard duty was anything like medicine, they'd tried to call someone in, but nearly everyone would be asleep at this hour. No one expected the Spanish Inquisition, and few expected urgent guard duty. Which meant that this trio would have to tough it out until the morning crew came on.

I hadn't verified the guards' work schedule, or really probed if Patrick had any enemies, but I could try again later. The ER worked like that. You had to take whatever information you could get, in quick bursts, before heading to the next patient, and the next.

I Googled +"security guards" +"St. Joseph's Hospital" +Montreal and was startled to uncover another news item from New Year's that I'd missed while transitioning from Ottawa to Montreal.

Maybe Patrick had more than one enemy.

Many question marks hung in the air: Julie. Jesse. Jason. Patrick's past. Alyssa's attack. Plus this new question of an "incident" on New Year's. Not to mention what happened to Ryan and the unusually silent Tucker.

"Are you okay?" asked a low female voice.

I turned and tensed when I saw who had spoken.

Roxanne tried to smile at me over the clipboard in her hands. "You still mad at me?" she said.

"I'm not mad."

"Sure you are."

I let the thought percolate through what was left of my brain. "Yes, but more frustrated. I wanted to do something for Patrick, not sit around with a thumb up my—you know."

"I know. This has been the worst night shift ever. I didn't want to block you from the code, but Dave thought it was the safest thing for you."

Uh oh. Tears welled behind my eyes. I had to turn away from her to suppress them. If nasty people lashed out at me, I reacted with controlled fury, but kindness undid me every time.

"We're still friends, right?" Roxanne reached for my hand.

I grabbed hers and nodded instead of talking. Less chance for weepage.

"Okay, then." She squeezed my fingers, released them, and sped away in her pink pant scrubs and sneakers, clipboard already raised in the air.

"Wait!" My voice broke.

She swivelled around to face me.

I hustled to her side so I didn't have to shout, conserving my voice. "I need to know what happened on Friday. Patrick was involved in that, right?"

Roxanne's face closed down. Dimples disappeared, eyelids at half mast, lips pursed. "That has nothing to do with anything."

"Still. What happened?"

She shook her head.

"There's that, and what happened on New Year's. I know Patrick had trouble with Lori Goody because he was afraid of another 'incident.' I'm trying to figure out what went on."

She twisted toward me and lowered her voice. "You heard about New Year's?"

"I saw it online when I looked up security at St. Joe's. The CBC interviewed an indigenous couple who said that four guards beat them up on New Year's. They didn't name the security guards, because they hadn't been charged yet and were only 'under investigation,' but I assumed that one of them was Patrick."

Roxanne's head dipped in acknowledgement as she held the clipboard in front of her chest, almost like armour. "I don't—I wasn't working that evening."

I waited. Her work status was irrelevant. She would have scooped up all the details regardless. I was an outsider, but no one would exclude Roxanne.

She licked her lips. "They weren't patients. They were friends visiting a patient on the unit, and they were all drinking and yelling and disturbing the other patients. You know what it's like."

Yep. The Intensive Care Unit existed as a mini-universe, blessed with one-on-one nursing care, where only a beeping monitor dared to interrupt the silence. It was a haven of quiet control, unlike the bedlam of the ER.

"So the other patients and families complained, and the nurses called the security guards. You know it's their job to walk out disruptive visitors. Or anyone else, like on Friday..." She closed her eyes and pressed a hand to her forehead.

I'd never seen Roxanne nearly break down like this. Every one of us rode close to the edge tonight. Her words confused me, though. "Wait. You said nothing happened on Friday."

She shook her head. "We're talking about New Year's. Never mind me, I'm tired." She flashed me a smile with some of her trademark spirit.

No, she hadn't convinced me. Something happened on Friday. I opened my mouth to press her.

She cut in first. "So anyway. On New Year's, we had four guards on. Double the usual staff ever since—"

Since 14/11. Yay.

"—that incident in OB." She supplied her own euphemism for the hostage taking, before moving on to New Year's. "Yes, Patrick was one of them. Actually, it was the same team as tonight. They went up to the unit. It was supposed to be no big deal, you know, jolly them up and walk them out of the hospital. They didn't think of calling the police because the couple seemed loud but not—dangerous, you know?"

"Right." I shuddered inside. When you weren't expecting a problem, it meant you weren't prepared for the worst. Ever since 14/11, I expected non-stop torment and brimstone.

"It was a man and a woman. The woman was so drunk that she kept falling down. Patrick tried to help her up. He was the tallest guard. I think he did that sort of thing a lot, but the drunk guy thought Patrick was hitting on his woman and swung at him. The other guards told the guy to get back, but he was like a bear. He jumped on Patrick and started whaling on him, too close together for the guards to get a clear shot with a taser. They got in with their batons—"

I recoiled. Steel batons.

"As soon as the guy got off Patrick, the guards put away their batons. They swear. But afterward, the guy said he was going to kill them. The woman screamed that they hated Indians. She cursed them out, said they were using racial slurs."

I exhaled. Although I couldn't imagine Patrick spewing hate, all bets were off when you were under attack. Exhibit A: me, tonight.

"The guards denied it, but they were scared. The guy went to UC four hours later. He ended up having two broken ribs and a hemo-pneumo."

I already knew that from the article. He said he couldn't breathe and ended up diagnosed with a punctured lung. The CBC obtained medical records showing that UC doctors had installed a chest tube and drained blood from around his lung. Those batons could have killed him.

"The couple got a lawyer. They went to the media. We don't know what's going to happen, except the hospital admin replied to the media and promised to get to the bottom of it. You know what that means."

It meant heads were going to roll. And not the CEO's head, but the underlings', because once again, shit rolls downhill. I closed my eyes, trying to process everything that had happened at St. Joe's during my research block in Ottawa. I hadn't gotten a whiff of it, even though I'd rejoined the ER this week.

I ignored everything except medicine when I was working, and residents were scattered around at various hospitals, post-vacation, but it struck me again that no one except Tucker and Tori truly talked to me.

It was possible that the guy had gotten the hemo-pneumo later, in between leaving St. Joe's and going to University College, but in another, more likely way, the guards could have killed him.

The guy thought Patrick had disrespected his woman. Patrick's buddies had broken his bones and busted his lung. The guy could try his luck with the courts, but they might not look favourably on a stereotypically drunk Indian. As in one of my favourite books, *To Kill a Mockingbird*, he might have decided that he had to create his own odds.

So did that man return tonight to shoot Patrick in the throat?

"Those batons," I said aloud. "They might not even have known how hard they were hitting. Batons are like having a bionic arm to beat people up."

Roxanne shook her head. "It's not that bad. They get training every year on how to use them. They know what they're doing."

Did they? I suspected that the police received more than an annual baton workshop. Patrick might have learned some techniques in his CÉGEP police course. Still, I couldn't imagine how they'd feel like experts with q 365 day training.

I shook my head. "I'm surprised they're allowed batons and tasers at all."

"Oh, in Montreal, the security guards pair up with the police. It's almost like they work as a team, because the police can't show up everywhere instantly. The guards practically live here."

Right. With one visitor beaten and one guard shot dead within ten days.

Still, I considered it a win that I could solidify two candidates on Patrick's enemy list: Julie's abusive boyfriend and the nameless New Year's visitor. "Did Patrick have any other enemies?"

"Not that I know of." She glanced at room 6 and scooped her clipboard off the table. "I'd better check some vitals."

"Sure. One last thing. Could you tell me what happened on Friday?"

Her face tightened.

20

"What's wrong?" I said.

Roxanne jabbed a pen behind her ear. "Don't worry about it. Listen, you look after yourself. I know that your ex is haunting you."

Huh? That came out of nowhere. "What are you talking about?" I never discussed Ryan at work. Even when he was my everything, he lived in Ottawa and rarely made it to the hospital. And now that I'd switched exclusively to Tucker, I tried not to let Ryan cross my consciousness.

Roxanne pressed on the clipboard clamp, opening and closing it on the piece of paper it contained. "I hope you're all right. I know that an ex can be...dangerous."

Wait. Was she saying what I thought she was saying? I cleared my throat. "Ryan would never hurt anyone, let alone me."

"Right." Her eyes rested on me in a way that guessed how I sobbed alone in the car. How I sometimes walked outside, by myself, at night, for hours, while Tucker slept, because I ached too much to lie beside him. How I tried to reconstruct Ryan's smell from a stolen sweater, or pulled out his letters and scanned his old messages.

Roxanne bit her lip and shook her head. "I'm not trying to judge, but we had a talk on intimate partner violence. Leaving your partner is the most dangerous time."

My brain silently exploded before I recovered my voice. "I *know* that. I said it to room 13 myself tonight. Ryan's not like that. He'd kill himself before he'd attack me."

Roxanne sighed.

"Okay, I know I have a few risk factors. Like my age, between 25 and 34. But Ryan never hit me"—*spanking doesn't count*—"in anger. He doesn't have a gun, he doesn't drink or take drugs. He's...annoyingly Christian. So don't worry about me and Ryan. Not that way." Coughing overtook me.

Roxanne patted me on the back. "I hope you're right."

We both laughed a little, because of my name, and she added, "I'm trying to look out for you, Hope."

"I appreciate that. Well, good luck with those vitals." I saluted her as she left, but couldn't relax until she'd cleared the Plexiglass walls. Man, that was bizarre.

Who told her about Ryan? I couldn't imagine Tucker confessing. He and Ryan practically incinerated each other when I tried to date both of them at the same time. Tori knew, but her lips were hermetically sealed. Although other residents were aware of our love triangle, most of them seemed too busy to gossip about us.

Ryan had picked me up once or twice at St. Joe's, so it was possible Roxanne had figured it out herself. I watched her slim body motor toward bed 13, and I wondered.

"Right on, Hope!"

When I turned around, Dr. Dupuis distracted me with a fist bump. "We did it!" Dr. Dupuis followed the fist bump with a finger explosion, so I belatedly joined in.

"We did?"

"Yes! There are no patients left to be seen!"

I checked my WOW. He was right. No one in the queue. He'd swept through the list like a chainsaw. No, like a forest fire. It was almost frightening, how fast the man could see patients, and do it well, unlike Dr. Callendar. I gave him his due. "You did it."

"Don't sell yourself short, Hope. You're my right hand woman who won't quit, even after a patient tries to strangle you. Now go get some sleep."

I glanced at the monitor to check if any of my results had come back, flagged by a white bar.

"If and when anything comes back, I'll deal with it. I know how to handle a knee film. Now go lie down." He hesitated. "Make sure you don't knock on the staff room door. Dr. Chia is, ah, having a rest."

I had to swipe my hand over my mouth to hide a smile. He loooooved her so much.

"I'll be out here. You know where to find me." He handed me the key on the two foot-long yellow handle.

"Thanks, chief." An unfortunate turn of phrase because it reminded me of the guards beating the indigenous man. My smile faded before I took the key in hand.

"What's wrong?"

I squeezed the wooden handle in my fist. Where should I begin? Patrick's death. His girlfriend's beating. A patient's visitor's beating. The constant ache of Ryan's absence, exacerbated by Tucker's muteness. The throbbing in my throat and neck.

I decided to zero in on the unanswered question. "What happened on Friday?"

"What?"

"Something happened here on Friday when I was in my clinic. Do you know what I'm talking about?"

Dr. Dupuis frowned at me. "Not really. Whatever happened is not as important as you getting some rest. Go." He pulled his phone out of his pocket like he was going to time me with the stopwatch.

"Fine." I strolled past the break room en route to my call room. The new nurse with the wavy blondish hair, Amber, raised wide eyes from her phone and shoved it in her pocket.

"You okay?" I said.

She shrugged. "I guess this is part of the deal?"

"I guess."

She sniffed and rubbed her long, freckled nose. "At least now I have battle scars."

"That's true." I was probably only a few years older than her, but I felt like an old roll of carpet ready to topple over. Meanwhile, she looked as wispy as candy floss. I wondered if she'd make it to next month, let alone next year. ER nurses are tough not only because the work hardens them up, but because the gentle lambs end up driven into more idyllic pastures. Say, a nice clinic that runs 8 to 4, with a wall to pin a picture of your kindergartener. "Sucks. Listen, I don't want to bother you, but did you work on Friday?"

She shook her head, pocketing her phone.

"Oh. Did you hear anything that happened on that shift? Especially involving Patrick, the guard who got shot?" It was a leading question, but I only had a few seconds before Dr. Dupuis might swoop down on us.

Her head tilted back. She pulled the elastic out of her hair and began braiding it. "Now that you mention it, Linda overheard a patient threaten him last week. I don't know what day it was—"

Who cared. I needed to add to my list of villains. "Who?"

Her eyes darted from side to side, and she dropped her voice, afraid someone might overhear us. "She didn't say much, except that it was this giant man who said he'd pop off...his balls and..."

Poor Amber. Her pale skin flushed as she struggled to repeat the words. Finally, she managed to whisper, "...chew them like candy."

"That is gross." And sort of creative. I'd never heard that one before.

"Linda said he laughed it off, but she could tell that it bothered him."

"That would bother anyone. I don't even have balls, and it makes me want to cross my legs."

Amber nodded and looped the elastic on the end of her neat braid.

"But a patient like that would be a Code White, right? Was he admitted? He might still be on the floor. And do you think Linda remembers his name?"

Amber shook her head. Her braid swung side to side. Her prominent nose and narrow face made her more gawky than pretty, which made me feel even more protective of her.

"Never mind. I'll ask Linda later. Thanks, Amber."

Once ensconced in the call room, shoes off, door locked and my body tucked into the single bed, I pulled off my glasses. I felt too tired to sit up and place my glasses on the desk, even though it was only two feet away from me. So close, and yet so far.

I sighed and placed my glasses beside the pillow, against the wall. "Try not to crush your own glasses," I instructed myself.

Then I closed my eyes, but my occipital lobe replayed Patrick's eyes, magnified by his own hyperopic lenses.

Patrick had been shot shortly after someone had attacked his girlfriend.

Patrick had made at least one enemy who'd been taken into custody. But I'd have to research Jesse and make sure he was still incarcerated. Even if he was behind bars, it was possible Jesse's friends could seek revenge, although that seemed less likely.

More recently, the guards had beaten an indigenous couple who were now bringing media attention to and legal action against St. Joe's.

And more specifically, a psychiatric patient had threatened Patrick's balls.

I tossed on my side, mindful not to squash my glasses. The plastic pillow cover crinkled under my ear, and I rolled again.

Then I sat up and started searching on my phone.

The indigenous gentleman, Curtis Hayden, came up immediately because of his media conference. Now I had the time to watch his video interview. He was a big guy, slightly overweight but in good shape, probably around 27, like me. He looked at the reporters who held a camera in his face and spoke to a woman with a curly bob.

Lou was crying. She was trying to get them off me. She tried to beat 'em, too, but I yelled at her, "Don't do it, just film the bastards, we'll put it on Twitter and let it go viral."

She got out her phone. One of 'em knocked it out of her hands, smashed it on the floor. Well, hell, that was our only phone, you know? Mine broke last month.

I lost it. I tried to pick up one guy, the old one, grabbed him by the crotch and shoulder. I was going to heave him out.

He had a baton. You know, those metal things? He whacked my ribs so hard, I just about passed out. Then he whacked me again, three, four times.

The other ones joined in. I could feel my ribs break. I heard 'em crack.

I yelled at Louisa to get out. I don't care what happens to me, but I can't let them hit her like that. She'd die. She's, uh, not very strong, you know? Me, I've been beat'n so many times, ever since I was a little kid. My dad, my uncle used to whale on me. They said that's how they make you a man. Anyway, I know how to take a beat'in'. I can take a lot.

She wouldn't go. She was crying, and she was screaming, "I'm gonna sue you."

I couldn't breathe. The last thing I heard was Lou screaming, "I'm gonna sue."

I would've laughed if I could've. But at the end, I couldn't do nothin'.

21

I closed my eyes. Curtis Hayden sounded like he was telling the truth.

The guards swore that they stopped hitting him as soon as he got off of Patrick.

The facts probably lay somewhere in between, but Curtis Hayden remembered them whacking him in the ribs, and he ended up with a documented hemothorax-pneumothorax. He'd probably win his case.

Curtis wouldn't get any money if he shot Patrick and bashed up his girlfriend and ended up in prison, right?

Unless he got so angry that he changed plans.

Would he resort to homicide? For Lou? It sounded like he loved her as fiercely as Dr. Dupuis loved Dr. Chia.

I know how to take a beat'in'. I can take a lot.

I drummed my fingers.

I couldn't reach out to Curtis Hayden easily. I was a doctor at St. Joe's, and therefore in the enemy camp. He'd gone to UC afterward, which was the trauma hospital, but maybe also because he never wanted to come back to St. Joe's.

All I could do was speculate. I shelved Curtis for now.

Then I switched villains.

Combing slowly through the Internet, zeroing in only on Montreal cases of beaten children, I found one man who had been convicted of beating a three-year-old—over a year ago. He'd been released before Christmas.

Would Jesse really wait one more month to kill one guy who'd stood up to him?

And would he try to choke Patrick's girlfriend as an appetizer?

It seemed far-fetched, but not impossible. The guy had beaten a three-year-old. I wouldn't put anything past him.

Switching to the third potential villain, the psychiatric patient, I'd have to quiz Linda to ferret out his name and piece together his location. For now, he'd uttered threats, but so would at least half the patients getting "walked out." The would-be ball-eater had come up with a more descriptive threat, no more. And of people who'd uttered threats, I'd guess that less than half would raise a hand at the time, let alone a week later. They were blowing off steam and saving face, not seriously announcing a dietary change to cannibalism.

However, Jesse and Curtis had both earned a spot on my list of suspects. Should I share this with the police?

Probably.

I called and got snared in voice mail hell. Montreal police had taken a leaf from Ottawa and were trying to avoid human contact. Eventually, I left a message and touched my camera icon so I could look at photos of Ryan.

Ryan had bought me my iPhone. In fact, he bought me two of them, after I lost the first on 14/11. This device was one of my last ties to him, not to mention my way to communicate with the outside world.

My phone buzzed with a text from Tucker:

He took the dog.

A single four-word text from Tucker, and my throat closed up again.

Ryan booked two weeks off work, and he took Roxy the Rottweiler. He was splitting a foster dog. It was complicated, but neither he nor his friend Rachel had much time to take care of a dog, so Ryan took Roxy 60 percent of the time. It wouldn't surprise me if he adopted her, because he adored her, but for the moment, she was still officially on the market. She could go anywhere.

She could leave him. Like me.

I tried to review this news rationally.

Ryan took Roxy. That meant he was planning to live, right? You don't take a dog if you want to off yourself. It would have been much easier to leave Roxy behind, with her other caretaker.

No, Ryan took Roxy somewhere.

On a trip?

Two more facts: Ryan blocked my phone number, and he wasn't answering his parents. He'd cut ties with the past.

It still made me dry heave, but when I tried to think dispassionately, like an engineer, it didn't sound slam dunk suicidal. It sounded like someone breaking free.

Ryan and Roxy would keep each other sane. Once, when we were disagreeing, Roxy started barking at us. We petted her. She lolled on the floor and pushed on Ryan with her paws before licking my wrist with her tongue, and Ryan and I laughed.

I feel about Ryan the way some people feel about hiking and running. He keeps me sane. And Roxy is now a part of that healing.

Tucker and I almost adopted an American dog together. That didn't work out. Someone else wanted him, a relative with a better claim, plus it made zero sense for us to own a dog. We can barely find clean underwear in the morning.

I exhaled.

I was at work. I couldn't leave my patients. Ryan was gone, but Tucker was proving his investigative talents by searching him out.

I had to trust both my guys and let go.

"Let go and let God," one of Ryan's churchy female friends once told me, while earnestly holding my hand and looking into my eyes.

"No, thanks," I'd said at the time, which hurt her feelings so much that I had to stop going to Ryan's church for a bit (world's smallest violin). But that was how I felt, creeped out and going for an automatic no.

I'd finally figured out what church girl was trying to tell me: if I couldn't do anything, then I wasn't responsible for it. I could relax and concentrate on looking after these patients in the ER.

So I still couldn't let go and let God. But maybe I could release my death talons on Ryan and let Tucker keep tabs on him. That, I could live with.

Before I turned back to the ER, I combed through social medial for Curtis.

ME AND MY POSSE! he'd posted at 1 a.m. It was a selfie at what looked like a bar.

Now, I know you can schedule posts. Social media is not a good alibi. But it was something. An idea where he was tonight, and that was definitely not the parking lot of St. Joe's—if I had the right guy, which is also never a hundred percent on social media.

But if I were a betting woman, I'd put my money on Jesse.

Did he do something on Friday? Did he enter St. Joe's, if not for Patrick, then for revenge against Julie?

And if so, where was she now?

22

I couldn't find Julie. I didn't even know her last name.

Andrea, who'd promised to play seeker, seemed to be on break.

Hark, the major pitfall of delegating: no guarantees the job would get done.

After pacing the ER, from the kitchen to the crash carts to triage and back again, I asked the secretary to keep an eye out for Julie. Then I ducked into room 13.

Alyssa had extended both arms to hold her phone above her face, an awkward position necessary because she was still lying flat on her back, neck immobilized in the C-collar.

I moved into her central vision so that she didn't have to shift her head to read my lips. "Hi Alyssa."

She placed the phone on the bed and forced the words out of her own bruised throat. "He's dead, isn't he."

It wasn't a question. Her eyes already knew. I took a deep breath and kept it simple. "Yes. We did everything we could, but we couldn't bring him back. I'm sorry."

"Because they shot him in the throat."

Maybe she'd read about it on the news or social media. Maybe someone texted her, or she overheard us talking at the nursing station. No matter how she'd figured it out, I nodded again. Sometimes, there are no words.

She closed her eyes and clenched her fists. The rage that electrified her body gave me the space to ask the key question. "Who did it, Alyssa?"

She started to shake her head from side to side.

"Please don't move your head until we clear your cervical spine, which I'll try to do as soon as we have nurses available. Please, Alyssa. Whoever shot Patrick—I bet it's the same people who attacked you. Luckily, your CT head was negative for bleeding, although it won't show a concussion. They fractured your nose and left cheekbone and almost ripped off your ear. Please tell us who did it. We'll protect you."

She choked back a laugh or a sob as her voice rasped, "That's the last thing you can do."

"Please. You have to trust us."

She squished her bruised eyes shut. I waited, tense. Alyssa could unlock the entire mystery for us, right here, right now.

She compressed the rest of her face. I had never seen anything like it, the brows and the mouth folding in on itself like origami, but I understood that this was her expression of grief. You're not allowed to scream in a hospital, her voice had been nearly choked out of her, and she had been stretched out like a modern day mummy while her lover was murdered.

"Get me *out* of here," she said.

"You're going to plastics at University College Hospital after 8 a.m. I can clear your C-collar if everything is normal. Give me a second."

"Get me out!" Her voice cracked.

"Just a second!"

I rushed out of room 13 and found Linda, who was in the middle of changing a dressing in bed 9, but I persuaded her to steady Alyssa's head while I removed the collar and checked her neck for any single point of tenderness.

"It's fine. I'm going home."

"Wait. Try to move your chin toward the ceiling and then back toward your chest. It doesn't have to be much. Whatever you can tolerate. Does this hurt? Do you have weakness, numbness, or tingling in your arms or legs?"

"No." She tried to sit up.

At least her neck truly didn't seem to bother her. "Alyssa, you're going to University College Hospital to meet plastic surgery after 8 a.m. You have to—"

"I'm getting out."

"No, Alyssa, you should get—"

She stood up, stumbled. Linda grabbed her on the left side, and I belatedly tried to support the other.

"It's not safe to go out there!" My voice splintered too. "We're kind of—well, two men tried to grab me in the parking lot, even before Patrick died—"

She made a wounded noise and pointed to her IV's. "Get these things out of me."

"Alyssa, I don't think you understand the risks of going home. Mentally and physically. Plastic surgery will take care of your facial fractures after 8 a.m.—"

She tried to rip the IV out of her left hand.

Linda covered the IV with her own palm and called, "You want to call a Code White?"

"NO!" Alyssa howled. It was the most dreadful sound she'd made, worse than when I told her Patrick died.

"I need some more Ativan," I said, catching a hold of Alyssa's right hand, but she clawed at me, nearly dislodging the IV in her right antecubital when it got hung up on my arm.

"I can't let go of her," said Linda.

"Agreed. Okay, I'll call a Code White." But when I opened my mouth to shout with the remnants of my vocal cords, Alyssa screwed her eyes shut and stopped twisting.

I paused, mouth agape. Alyssa's arms and legs had gone rigid. Her wrist trembled under my fingers. For a second, I thought she might be seizing, normal CT notwithstanding. But when tears leaked out of her eyes, I understood that anguish had conquered her body.

We waited, our hands gentler now, but still resting on each arm while her muscles shook, reminding me of a trapped horse.

I felt like a torturer. I could hardly speak. "I'm sorry. I'm sorry for you and Patrick."

She shook and shook and shook.

"I can get that Ativan," said Linda, but I shook my head. As soon as she left for meds, Alyssa might pluck those IV's out and deliver an uppercut to my jaw.

"Could you get another nurse in here with the Ativan?" I murmured. "A milligram should do it." I couldn't have her either too wild or too sedated for plastics.

"I'm good. I don't need drugs," Alyssa whispered.

It broke my heart that she said she was good. In old movies, they often either slapped "hysterical" patients or tranquilized them. We didn't slap people anymore, and we only tranquilized if necessary. Yet she needed help so badly, and I didn't have the time or proper training for counselling. I couldn't leave her like this.

"Just let me out of here. I have to go home. Please." She blinked back tears. She couldn't wipe them because we were imprisoning her.

If Ryan or Tucker had been killed, I would want to go home too. And plastics probably wouldn't operate on her today. Even if they did, as long as she were fasting, she didn't have to wait in the emergency room, since her C-spine had been cleared.

I made a snap decision. "Alyssa, the safest thing is to stay here. But even if you go home, you need someone who'll stay with you and watch you for signs of head injury. You may also not feel safe in your apartment, since that's where you were injured. Is there someone you can call to come get you in the middle of the night?"

"My sister. Karen."

"Okay. Call Karen. She'd have to take you to University College Hospital for 8 a.m. You'd hardly get home before you'd turn right around, and it's safer here. The police might want to talk to you, too, so I can't promise anything—"

"Please!"

"I have to talk to Dr. Dupuis, too. He's the consulting physician on today."

Despite the tears glimmering on her eyelids, a smile poked at the corner of her lips. "God."

I couldn't resist a half-grin back. Even a security guard's previously healthy girlfriend knew who St. Joe's "God" was. "Yeah. We have to listen to God, okay? Let me go get him. It won't take long." With any luck, he wasn't simultaneously running codes on five different floors.

"I have to go home," she whispered, but quietly. Her torso began to vibrate again as she reached for her phone. Linda wrapped an arm around her in support while I hurried out in search of a tall, stork-like attending physician.

Medically, Alyssa should stay here, but it was psychological torture to stay at the hospital where her boyfriend had been shot. Maybe I could persuade UC to take her early, even though no one wants a transfer in the wee hours of the morning, and the ambulances are often too tied up for routine transportation.

I hustled toward the nursing station entrance across from room 14, eyes raised to catch a six footer in a lab coat, when a certain stillness caught the corner of my eye.

Across from me, a man-mountain dressed in 100 percent black stood in the hall outside the resuscitation rooms, blocking the opposite opening to the nursing station.

He could have been a patient, but it was less likely in all his winter outdoor gear. The ambulance patients changed into blue gowns, all the better to wear cardiac monitors. The walk-in patients, who often didn't require a gown, clustered in the waiting room before they were shuttled, one at a time, into exam rooms. They left through the doors that opened directly into the hallways.

No fully dressed patients headed into the heart of the ER, toward resus and the nursing station, unless they were lost or searching for a family member.

I hadn't forgotten my mission to find Dr. Dupuis.

But somehow, I couldn't wrench my eyes away from this giant

shrouded in black, from the balaclava over his face and the wool coat covering his massive body right down to his ankles, and black boots.

Maybe the would-be kidnappers in the parking lot had turned me against the colour, but he made my skin prickle.

My gaze dropped down to his round-toed, heavy-soled lace-up boots, trying to figure out if these were the same pair I'd stomped on in the parking lot, but my memory balked, too clouded by fogged-up glasses, night, snow, and fear.

"What's happening, Hope?" Linda called.

I couldn't linger. Alyssa might flip at any moment.

Still, my breath hitched and told me this guy was danger. Danger, danger, danger.

"Can I help you?" I yelped.

His head slowly rotated toward me. He seemed to be wearing some sort of Bluetooth headset with a mouthpiece next to his masked lips.

I tried to stand with my feet apart, grounding me on the tile floor, making me appear confident despite my frail voice. My memory pinged, trying to grasp something distantly familiar, as I reviewed his features beneath the knit mask and the coat cloaking his potato body shape.

He moved stiffly, almost robotically. His shoulders twisted to follow his head before the rest of his body followed suit. Maybe he really was hurt and I'd misjudged an overdressed patient.

Still, the punk rock secretary glanced up from the phone, since he hovered only three feet away from her left elbow. Andrea and a nurse I didn't know looked up from their terminals at the nursing station.

A door closed on the ambulatory side. An IV pump beeped from one of the beds.

The man spoke next, his voice electronically distorted and amplified. "I have a bomb."

23

The secretary threw her hands in the air like he'd ordered a stick 'em up. "Did you say—a bomb?"

"I have a bomb," he repeated, in that same creepy electronic voice that deadened all expression. *It is snowing outside. It is Sunday, January twelfth. I have a bomb.*

A motherfucking bomb.

He could've been joking around. Twice. *He's the bomb.*

But my gut screamed that this man wouldn't hesitate to annihilate us.

I'd been held hostage less than two months before. Gun to my head in the labour and delivery room. What were the odds?

Unless this was a copycat threat.

I heard there's this great hospital. All you have to do is break in and try to kill everyone. Nothin' like it. You in?

Yeah. But let's do it bigger and better. Forget one room with a gun. Let's do the whole ER with a bomb. Yeah?

Yeah!

The criminals had started playing Clue, only instead of Professor Plum in the library with a rope, I'd lucked out with Colonel Black in the ER with a bomb.

I felt too tired for gibbering terror. Seriously. After a while, you're so numb that dropping dead seems like a reasonable Door Number Three.

"Okay. You have a bomb," I said. Forget denial, rage, and heart-break. I'd skated straight to acceptance. This was the worst night shift of my life. Of course a man would cap it off with a bomb. The key was to survive said bomb. "Can we move all the patients out of here?"

After a pause, Bomb Guy intoned, "No."

Okay. *May* we move all the patients out of here? But I suspected Bomb Guy wasn't a grammar Nazi. He simply wanted to exterminate every one of us.

Well, it was worth a shot (no pun intended). And his response told me that he was able to modulate his voice in real time, instead of repeatedly pressing a recording that said, *I have a bomb.*

Still, he wanted something. If his only goal was devastation, he should have walked straight in and detonated the bomb. Instead, he'd spoken to us. Warned us.

"What do you want?" I called. The effort made me cough, and I hacked into the crook of my elbow, keeping my hands up to show that they were empty.

"Give me your drugs. Narcotics and benzos."

He was naming them by drug class. Nobody I know does that unless they work in the medical field.

Bomb Guy was one of us.

Not Jesse or Curtis, then. I supposed the psychiatric patient could have learned the medication classes, but my instincts whispered to look closer to home.

"I'm—I don't know how to unlock the medication cart," I said. "You need a badge to unlock it. I'm not authorized."

"Well, then, you're a useless piece of shit, aren't you." The electronic voice couldn't convey expression, but something about the rhythm of his words told me he derived great pleasure from telling me so. More than a stranger would.

This guy was probably from St. Joe's.

Who the hell was he?

I studied his face as best I could through the eyeholes of his bala-clava. Even from a distance, I noted pale skin, greasy with sweat. So he was a white guy who didn't relish this.

The main thing, though, was his build. Part of his body habitus might be the bomb he was carrying—surely it would add twenty pounds to any svelte silhouette—but he looked a good 250 pounds to me.

"One of the nurses. You. Amber." He pointed at the new nurse who'd gotten bitten.

She'd been hovering in room 14, behind me. She squeaked.

"Go get the drugs. Morphine, Fentanyl, Dilaudid, Versed, Ativan. All of it. Now."

Amber's lips quivered. She ducked her head and her entire body, almost like she wanted to kowtow.

Amber was new. I'd never worked with her before tonight, yet he knew she was a nurse. Sure, he could have read her badge, except he didn't hesitate. He named her immediately. And he'd chosen her over two more experienced nurses already frozen inside the nursing station.

I might know who Bomb Guy was.

We had never liked each other, but this was beyond anything I'd ever considered him capable of.

"Do it, Amber. Unless you want this." He placed a hand to his chest. He must be wearing an explosive vest.

Amber scurried toward the resus room, body still bowed like a candy cane. Probably she didn't want to look him in the eye. Probably a smarter tactic than me chatting, but my only weapon was my mouth. Unless he got close enough for my scalpel.

"She'll have to enter patient names to get the drugs out of the system. I can help her!" Andrea called from her spot at the nursing station, closer to bed 3.

"Don't you move. No one else fuckin' moves a muscle. That kid gets my drugs, and the rest of you play freeze tag. Stay right where you are, or I will blow up this hospital." He headed straight for room 14 without even checking the room sign above the door.

When he passed me, I held my breath but didn't dare stir.

Room 14.

Our psych room, and the room that used to contain Lori Goody.

He drew back the curtain with a practiced hand. At minimum, he was a frequent flyer patient or visitor. This man not only knew his drugs, he knew St. Joe's uncomfortably well.

The demented patient now occupying room 14 issued an angry yell.

Bomb Guy stepped right out and back to his spot next to the secretary. "Where is she?"

So he was searching specifically for Lori Goody. She had managed to give him her room number despite being physically and chemically subdued during a Code White.

They certainly deserved each other, and it made sense now: he wasn't randomly cleaning out our stash. He was handing drugs over to his girlfriend/pal/thing.

"How did you know she was there?" I whispered.

His eyes flickered.

Recognition crept along my spine. He was big. He was surly. He was even still hanging out near the resuscitation rooms.

"Bill?"

He didn't answer, but he didn't deny the name, either.

Bill. The fat, angry male nurse who used to sit beside resus most of the time. The one Kris had said was *gone. He's done.*

Why hadn't Kris been more specific? "Done" could mean anything from "He's working at the Jewish Hospital" to "He flew to Tahiti."

Had Bill grabbed me in the parking lot? No wonder me stomping his foot hadn't made a dent in this colossus. Now he'd returned to flay me.

I shook that off and pretended to be pals. "We didn't have a chance to get to know each other. I've been away for a month on a research block." I figured that if I spoke normally, like we were buddies, he was less likely to blow us all to hell.

"Where's Lori?" he repeated, in his mechanical voice.

Right. He didn't care about my research in a stem cell lab, only about Lori Goody. How could I work that? Not sure, but while I tried to puzzle that one out, I told him the truth. "She's at the Glen. That's her sector."

His eyes blinked at me behind his mask. He didn't ask what the Glen was, or what a sector meant. He understood immediately that she'd been sent to the Montreal superhospital, further confirming my suspicions. Except his next words made my heart thump. "No. Roxanne said she was here."

24

The secretary and nurses wheeled around to stare at Roxanne, who had crossed into the nursing station from the entrance near bed 2.

Now we formed a triangle: Bomb Guy at one entrance at 10 o'clock, Roxanne at 2 o'clock, and me at 6 o'clock. The secretary quivered between Bomb Guy and Roxanne. Andrea and the older nurse I didn't know sat between Roxanne and me.

"That's old information," I said, trying to glue Bomb Guy's eyes to mine, even though my brain screamed at the idea that Roxanne had fed him any kind of inside scoop.

I'd felt betrayed when Roxanne blocked me from helping Patrick, but I'd understood it. This, I would never understand.

Unless he was lying. Yes, that seemed far more likely. Although how he'd figured out Lori Goody's room number—

"You're both right," said Roxanne. I'd never appreciated the melodiousness of her low voice before this appalling moment. She faced me, cheeks slightly flushed like her pink scrub pants, before she angled herself toward Bomb Guy. "I told you when Lori came in. She's gone now, though. She's safe."

"She's not fucking safe. You're putting her through hell." His mechanical voice made the swears almost comical, but his bomb kept my amusement in check.

"We're trying to help her," I told him.

"You have no clue what that means," he replied, eyes stabbing me. The voice changer made me envision a robot faulting me for insufficient empathy. "You're an idiot. I told my sister."

His sister? Who would have thought that obese Bill would have such a skinny sister. It was like Jack Sprat could indeed eat fat, and his sister Lori was naught but lean.

Bill informed me, "It's the nurses who hold this place together."

I knew what he meant. I write the orders, but the nurses usually have to unlock the medications, draw them up, and administer them. They literally hold the patients' hands, relieving their pain and cleaning them up.

That's why when patients come to the hospital, they don't remember the doctors who jab them with needles, cut them open, or wrench their bones into place. Or they often don't remember us fondly.

They remember the nurses who go hands-on to make them feel better.

On the other hand, someone has to slave away at school for a minimum of 22 years for the privilege of issuing orders and getting sued. So we work as a team, along with people like Julie. She fetches them crutches so they can walk again, and feeds Grandma if she's too weak to hold the spoon.

Not a good time to lecture Bomb Guy about #squadgoals, though. I agreed, "Nurses are very important."

"What's happening?" called the old, male patient from bed 6. No one answered him.

"Bill," Roxanne cut in, taking two steps toward him.

Gasps echoed through the ER. I'd made the hypothesis about his identity. Maybe others had recognized him, but had held their tongues, hoping that he'd steal the drugs and leave, much like tossing your wallet to a mugger.

Now Roxanne had confirmed the bomber's identity and, I

suspected, her own complicity. Earlier tonight, she'd recognized Lori as his sister and kept him in the loop. Then Roxanne had deliberately ducked my inquiries about Friday night, feeding me questions about Ryan instead of telling me that Patrick had walked Bill out.

What had I said at the beginning of the night? *Do not mess with nurses. They will stick together and mess you up.*

I never expected them to bomb me, though. Florence Nightingale, where art thou?

Bomb Guy Bill lifted his black-gloved palm in the air. "Get out of here, Roxanne. I don't want to hurt you."

Uh oh. Automatic translation: *I want to hurt everyone else.*

Roxanne's sneakers stilled, although her hands stretched toward him. "I don't want you to hurt anyone, Bill. Please. I'll help you and your sister get what you need. Then you can go, right?"

Bill paused before he answered. I'd noticed a slight lag before his live responses, presumably to mechanize his voice, but this pause was long enough for him to consider scooping the drugs and running.

Good idea, Bill.

Then his robo voice kicked in. "I only need one more thing. Where's Lori?"

"She went to the Glen."

I relaxed slightly. Roxanne had stuck to the facts, corroborating me, so now he knew I'd told him the truth. *No reason to bomb us, Bill.*

"With the police?" he asked.

Roxanne licked her lips. She lowered her hands to her sides, not wanting to piss him off, but unable to lie. "Yes."

"FUCK." His robot voice couldn't convey emotion, but it could and did blast us with sheer volume.

Roxanne's narrow shoulders jerked as if he'd hit her.

Bill said, "Sorry."

An apology! I grew still, watching him for any other sign of humanity.

"I want Lori here," he added.

Everyone comes to the emergency room because they want something. Remember that, a female emergency doctor had instructed me in medical school. Bill had repeatedly named his big two: free drugs and Lori Goody. We could hand him the first one, but not the second. Maybe Roxanne could placate him.

"My sister comes back with me, or I'm detonating this." He tapped his chest again.

Or not.

If nothing else, he kept confirming the location of his bomb. Unfortunately, I knew almost nothing about explosive vests except that suicide bombers wore them. And what if he'd rigged up a dirty bomb?

A med student who'd worked in Israel as an ambulance driver had told me about his first dirty bomb. First the bomb itself had exploded, and then it launched some extra surprises. "There was this girl, a beautiful teenager, holding up her hand. A nail had gone through her palm. But we couldn't pick her up because there were other people who were hurt worse than that."

In addition to nails and screws, which could lodge in your eye or up your yoni, Bill could have added some hepatitis-infected needles. Or blood, urine, feces, or vomit. The only limit was his imagination and his willingness to strap it to his chest.

I bet he'd looked after Lori since they were kids. Their blood ties ran deeper than girlfriend or wife. He really would kill us if we didn't serve her up.

Solution: give him Lori. Or at least promise her to him. I opened my mouth, but a man's voice behind me and to my left, at 8 o'clock, spoke first.

"We'll get Lori to you as soon as humanly possible."

Dr. Dupuis had exited his ambulatory exam room, quietly closing the door of room 4 behind him. "We can help you with this. You have to give us time to get her here."

I started flashing back to 14/11—woman panting in labour, gun firing—and fought it hard, trying to ground myself with concrete details. Right now, I could smell wet wool. I could see a man sweating under a balaclava and a full length coat. I could hear the IV pump still beeping and taste the remnants of butterscotch in my mouth.

I was in an emergency department with patients, staff, and at least three different exits. With God. I wouldn't pin all my wishes and dreams on him, because I've had to haul my own ass out of the fire every. Single. Time.

Still, if I had to choose getting bombed with God or without God, of course I'd choose God!

We outnumbered Bomber Bill. I'd rarely seen the guy walk, let alone run. Mentally, he was a few fries short of a full meal deal. We might be able to take him.

His only ace was the bomb he claimed to have.

And possibly Roxanne. I couldn't trust her any more.

We could call Bomber Bill's bluff. He'd been fired less than 48 hours ago. What were the chances that he'd managed to build a real, effective bomb in that period of time?

On the other hand, he might have stolen some dynamite from a construction site. I heard gangs did this back when the mafia ran everything in Montreal. Plus it was supposed to be easy to build explosives using instructions online or in a physical book.

If I challenged Bill and he really did have a bomb, we'd all lose. Instantly. Even those not in immediate range could be taken down by shrapnel or a collapsing building.

And our patients were so debilitated, it wasn't like they could jump out of bed and flee.

No, we'd have to play the safe game, give him the drugs, and pretend to gift wrap Lori Goody.

"Let me call the Glen," I said, nice and loud. For once, my voice obeyed me.

Dr. Dupuis cut in. "Hang on."

I enunciated my words to Dr. Dupuis, trying to convey my plan. "They don't know that Bill is looking for Lori. We need to contact the Glen by phone right now, okay?"

God glared at me.

I raised my eyebrows back at him. God should understand that we desperately needed to communicate with the outside world. We should summon the bomb squad ASAP. As long as Bill kept us as silent, still hostages, no one would know to come rescue us.

With luck, a patient or a staff member not immediately in Bill's line of sight had already called 911.

I couldn't bet on it, though. My only sure-fire way was pressing 911 with my own fingers. And contacting Lori Goody guaranteed me phone access.

"I can call them right now," I said. "I know the phone number." *Please don't keep me on hold.* "I'll call her unit, tell them I was her treating physician—"

"You're a baby." Bill glared at me. "You're a resident. They'll need Dave."

I'd take insulting me over exploding my body into microscopic bits. Even so, I struggled to keep my face expressionless.

"I'm right here," said Dr. Dupuis, walking toward Bill. Maybe he'd caught on to my plan. "I'm happy to negotiate—"

"No. No negotiation. Either she's here in the next 45 minutes, and we both get out safely, or you're all going down."

"I'll talk to them. I'll tell them exactly what you said. You can listen to make sure." Dr. Dupuis looked him straight in the eye. Maybe they could get their man/buddy/friend vibe going. Whatever worked.

Bill rolled his neck from side to side. The balaclava and wool coat and explosive vest and boots probably kept him uncomfortably toasty, but he met Dr. Dupuis's eyes for a good fifteen seconds. Finally, he said, "You talk to them in front of me. You put it on speakerphone. You say one wrong thing, and it's over."

"Understood," said Dr. Dupuis. "I'm pressing zero now. I want to talk to the operator."

If it was anything like St. Joe's, that would only net him the security guard replacing the operator overnight.

I brightened. An alert security guard would come in handy right now.

Bill's eyes darted toward me, and I tried to mask my emotion. Author Elizabeth Gilbert's friend once said that instead of a poker face, Liz had a "miniature golf face." Bill didn't dig my miniature golf face.

"Hi. This is Dr. Dave Dupuis at St. Joseph's Hospital. I need to talk to the psychiatrist on call, stat. I repeat, psychiatry. Stat."

"Lori Goody," said Bill's mechanical voice.

"I need you to transfer a patient named Lori Goody. Stat. No, I can't explain it to you. We need Lori Goody at St. Joseph's Hospital on Cote-des-Neiges. We have a Code Black—"

Bill knocked the phone receiver out of Dr. Dupuis's hand. Then he whacked him on the head with it.

Dr. Dupuis tried to cover his head, or at least his glasses, but made no other move to defend himself.

The plastic phone case splintered, exposing cables and what looked like a circuit board.

Someone sucked her breath in. No one dared scream.

This could be it. The final seconds of our lives, watching God get smashed in front of us.

God made no sound, although I could see the marks on his hands. His glasses bounced on the floor.

I tensed, forcing myself to stand still.

Once the phone case split into thirds, Bill ripped the phone cable out of the wall and held it up to Dr. Dupuis's throat.

"You fucker. I'm going to kill you."

25

"Wait a minute! I have something to tell you about Lori," said Dr. Dupuis, his hands in the air to ward off throttling. He squinted, face naked, without his glasses.

"You think I don't know what a Code Black is, motherfucker. It means a bomb. If that dumb fuck figures it out—"

"You're right. I'm sorry. It's about your sister, Lori—"

"Shut up. You weren't even on duty when she came in. I want Chia."

The ER fell silent, apart from the IV beeping and the hiss of a solitary blood pressure cuff.

"Valerie Chia," said the electronic voice, as Bill twisted the cord around each of his hands to get a better grip on it. *All the better to strangle you with, my dear.*

I felt light-headed staring at his black form. Physically, Bill could squish me. Hell, he'd already taken on God—not that God had fought back, for fear of the bomb, but Bill had demonstrated that he was as strong as a gorilla and willing to take down our leader.

Except Dr. Dupuis would never give up Dr. Chia.

He'd kept her inside the building until daylight to protect her. Instead, she was trapped in the epicentre.

Dr. Dupuis lowered his hands and spoke evenly. "You can't have Dr. Chia."

"I have a bomb."

Dr. Dupuis's expression never wavered. He didn't answer.

Bomb Guy tossed the phone cord to the floor, causing the secretary to squeal, before he raised his hands toward his chest.

We all tensed. One woman sobbed.

I don't want to die like this.

I love you, Tucker.

I love you, Ryan.

I love you, Kevin. Take care of Mom and Dad.

"Bill, please!" Roxanne cried.

Bill reached inside his coat, toward his left armpit.

Bombers often placed detonators in their pockets. The armpit seemed like a bad choice, since he could accidentally press the trigger by adducting his arm to his chest. What the—?

He withdrew a black pistol from a shoulder holster, aiming it at Dr. Dupuis's forehead. "Bring Dr. Chia here. Now."

This close, Bill wouldn't miss. He placed both hands on the grip, left hand reinforcing his right. He knew what he was doing, unlike actors posing one-handed on TV.

I'd take a gun over a bomb, but not by much.

You can't shoot Dr. Dupuis. You can't shoot God.

But I'd witnessed other people cut down in front of me before. Denial wasn't protection. It only made you die surprised instead of resigned.

I sent silent thanks that I'd sent Tucker away. *Thank you, Ryan, for getting him out of the city. You have both escaped the death vortex that is Hope Sze.*

Although I'd outlived other killers, this one was the most armed. My best chance of survival was the bomb squad.

Dr. Dupuis had managed to alert the Glen's secretary or security guard that we had a Code Black. But that person had to recognize a

Code Black and notify the police, who might hem and haw before dispatching someone to another hospital.

Too many moving parts. I itched to call 911 myself. Cut out the middleman.

But as soon as the Glen said "St. Joe's," officers should go on high alert. The police had barely left. Patrick had been shot and I'd nearly been nabbed. It should only take a few minutes for the bomb squad to liberate us.

Which meant that Bomb Guy had to act immediately, or not at all. He needed Dr. Chia now. The longer we dithered, the higher the chance that she could escape, or that the cavalry would bust our doors.

Which drove up the risk that we'd all get blasted to pieces.

I heard footsteps on the tile behind me. Light, hesitant footsteps. I didn't dare turn around. What if a patient had decided to run interference while Bomb Guy threatened to punch a bullet through Dr. Dupuis's famous brain?

The footsteps stopped.

Bomb Guy kept his gun fixed on Dr. Dupuis, but he snarled out of the corner of his mouth, "What are you doing."

A woman's voice whispered behind me, "Doctor's in the call room."

26

Someone had ratted out Dr. Chia.

A woman.

Shocked silence, followed by somebody moaning in disbelief.

Not me. I held on to my breathing and followed the gun, remembering what Officer Visser told me: *police officers watch hands, not faces. The hands are what's going to kill you.*

"Say it again," instructed Bomb Guy, still holding his gun at Dr. Dupuis. God's nostrils flared, but otherwise, he stayed statue-still.

"Dr. Chia is in the call room," said the woman more distinctly.

I knew this voice.

I revolved my head a few degrees to the left so I could identify the traitor.

Julie, the little preposée, held her arms in the air.

I'd agonized about her and her son. Andrea had tried to root her out. Now Julie had reappeared in time to help Bill.

Roxanne—deep down, I didn't believe that Roxanne would hurt us.

But I hardly knew Julie. Bill might have worked with her for years, might even have tried taking over Jesse's empty role.

What if Julie had gone AWOL while she helped Bill navigate past the metal detectors and security guards?

Hell, suicide bombers often have handlers who shepherd them into place, encouraging them to press that little button because it's a far, far better thing they do.

Sometimes the handler triggers the explosion through a cell phone or another wireless device. Makes sense when you think about it. Enough suicide bombers probably back out at the last second, but the handler has fewer hang ups about making the bomber and everyone else go boom.

What if *Julie* had masterminded this?

What had she said at the beginning of the night, about Dr. Chia's lottery win? *Better than getting walked out.* I'd assumed she meant an unruly patient like Lori Goody, but maybe she'd referred to the security guards escorting Bill out of the building.

No, Julie wasn't going to get walked out. She'd toss us in the fire first.

"Julie!" Dr. Dupuis snapped.

She ignored him. "You know where the call rooms are? Down there." She pointed to her right, down the shadowed hall. "There's the break room on the right first, with no door. Then you have a door on each side. The staff one is on the right. The one with the shower. So check the first closed door on your right, the one with a combination lock."

"A lock," Bomb Guy repeated.

That combination lock was the final, flimsy barrier between him and Dr. Chia.

Even I didn't know the code to the staff room.

We all watched Dr. Dupuis.

Bomb Guy's hands didn't shake. He had better arm stamina than me as he held the gun between Dr. Dupuis's eyes.

"The code to the door," Bomb Guy repeated in his electronic voice, "or I'll shoot you."

"I don't care if you shoot me. I'd rather be dead than give her up," said Dr. Dupuis evenly.

Bomb Guy gave a robotic heh heh. "Oh, I wouldn't kill you first. I'd shoot you in the knees. That's what the IRA did, right."

I shuddered. The electronic laugh. The flat tone. It made it even more obvious that he didn't care about us and would, in fact, enjoy torturing us along the way.

Dr. Dupuis's shoulders and legs braced, ready to jump him. If I could see it from twenty paces, Bomb Guy must, too.

"I wouldn't do that," said Bomb Guy, right hand tucking inside his right coat pocket.

The detonator!

We watched Bomb Guy keep the gun up with his left hand while his right stayed on the detonator.

Dr. Dupuis's hands fisted.

Bomb Guy's non-dominant hand held the gun. We could fight him for it. But the bomb kept us all motionless.

"I won't give you the code," said Dr. Dupuis.

"Yeah, maybe you wouldn't, but someone else will. How 'bout that gook?" He waved the gun at me.

I hit the cold tile floor on my stomach. I have a healthy respect for handguns and all things lethal.

Bomb Guy laughed. "Yeah, she's a real hero. All those newspaper articles, all those blogs talking up 'the detective doctor,' and this is where she ends up: kissing the floor."

I'd rather kiss this MRSA-laden floor than your racist ass, I thought, but as long as he was laughing and not shooting or detonating, I could put up with a few more insults.

My abdominal wall pushed against the floor as I breathed in and out, racking my brain for options. I still wanted to call 911, but I didn't dare now that he was focused on me.

"All right, bitch, give me the code."

"I don't know it. The residents use the other call room. We unlock it with the key on the yellow stick."

"Yeah? You never played doctor in the staff room with this guy?"

My eyebrows hitched up to my hairline. I've never thought of Dr. Dupuis that way. God is asexual. To me, anyway.

"Forget it. I'll shoot the lock off." His hand tightened on the trigger, which he aimed back at Dr. Dupuis. "Kill you, shoot the lock off, grab Chia and the meds. Done."

He was thinking out loud. It meant he didn't have much of a plan.

If Julie had been in on it from the beginning, she could have led him to the back door of the staff room, which I believed opened into the hallway, like mine. Or she could have figured out some way to unlock the conference room. Bomb Guy could have busted in through either door, and Dr. Chia might not even have had a chance to scream.

Unless Julie hadn't figured out Dr. Chia's whereabouts until now. Maybe Julie had been roaming the hospital, searching for Dr. Chia while Bomb Guy figured out how to strap dynamite to his chest.

One thing I knew for sure: Julie hadn't grabbed me in the parking lot. Too small, too female.

If Bomb Guy had been one of the two parking lot kidnappers— and using Occam's Razor, he would be—then his buddy waited somewhere. They'd tried to seize me, then shot Patrick.

I pushed myself up like I was doing cobra pose in yoga and glanced over my shoulder. No second man in black, but that didn't mean squat.

I did catch Julie out of the corner of my eye. Mouth open. Her hands quivered in the air.

She wanted no part of this.

Maybe she hadn't let Bomb Guy in. Maybe Roxanne had. Or, more likely, nobody did. You can always find an unlocked back door into a hospital, and he might have an old ID card that still worked.

Still, Julie couldn't give him more precise directions to Dr. Chia unless she'd taken him by the hand and offered him an aperitif along the way. She didn't give a gob about her, or us.

She'd sacrifice anyone, as long as she got out alive.

I might think that way, too, if I had a kid. I don't know. But I felt searing contempt for her. So much for the St. Joe's "family."

"I have to go to the bathroom!" called an elderly voice from eight o'clock.

Bomb Guy issued an electronic laugh, probably because he was relieved (har har) that he no longer had to attend to patients' bodily functions.

While he was distracted by hilarity, I reached for the phone in my front pocket and tucked it under my stomach so I could surreptitiously press and hold the power and a volume button with my right hand.

Like I'd told Alyssa, that would eventually alert EMS.

First it activates an SOS on the screen for you to swipe right, but I didn't dare bob my head again to check the screen. Risky enough that I'd hidden a hand under myself like I was reaching for my goods.

One Mississippi.

Two Mississippi.

Bomb Guy had stopped laughing.

"The heartbeat of Côte-des-Neiges" would arrest at any moment. As soon as he pressed the detonator.

"Okay, time to take out a kneecap," said Bomb Guy, sounding almost cheerful as he pulled his hand out of his pocket in order to steady the pistol.

"You don't want to do this." Roxanne sounded like she was going to cry.

That made Bomb Guy's head shift toward her, and then he noticed my missing hand.

"What the *fuck* are you doing?"

Five Mississippi.

Bomb Guy strode toward me, cutting through the nursing station.

Nurses and the secretary half-screamed and ducked under countertops.

Meanwhile, I scrambled to my feet. I would not lie on the ground for him to execute me.

"What the fuck am *I* doing?" he asked himself, and then he pulled the trigger on me.

27

I hit the deck a second time. I hadn't made it two feet.

Am I dead?

Tucker had told me that he didn't feel the pain right away when he was shot. First the impact, then the pain.

I didn't feel anything except the cold floor under my stomach. My teeth chattered, partly from the cold and partly from the shock. I was still within the Plexiglass walls of the nursing station, ten feet away from Bomb Guy's shoes.

Where did he get me? How long would it take for me to bleed out?

"Don't shoot her! Don't shoot her!" Faintly, I heard Dr. Dupuis's frenzied command and everyone else's screams before Bomb Guy's electronic shouts overtook them.

"All of you, on the floor with your hands over your heads! Now!"

I obeyed, even though my ears rang and my head spun.

Yes, it made sense to keep all of us helpless and on the ground while he killed me, kneecapped Dr. Dupuis, shot off the lock and grabbed Dr. Chia. I wanted to keep an eye on him, but my own surrendered hands blocked my peripheral vision.

"Get down." Bomb Guy's electronic bellow penetrated my injured tympanic membranes.

Again: "Get *down!*"

He was ordering God. I knew it. Dr. Dupuis wouldn't drop to the floor, because then Bomb Guy would feel free to abduct Dr. Chia.

Slight pause before electronica kicked in again: "I don't want to kill you."

Hey, no fair. Bomb Guy had felt perfectly fine about shooting *me*. Bang bang, Hope's dead!

Only I wasn't. As far as I could tell, he'd missed.

And, since no one else had cried out, maybe he'd missed deliberately. It was more of a warning shot.

God spoke. "You don't want to do this. You don't want Val. She's your friend."

"You have no idea what I want," Bomb Guy replied mechanically.

"Yes, I do. We've worked together since I was a resident. That's what, sixteen years?"

Bomb Guy didn't answer.

"Bill," said Dr. Dupuis, "you know I was here Friday—"

"You didn't do jack shit. No one did. They walked me out. They even handcuffed me!"

Wow. That was extreme. How'd they get that one past the union? The nurses' union is almost bulletproof. During the probation period, admin can let you go, but otherwise, the nurses will fight and fight to be reinstated or, at the very least, terminated without penalty.

Why did Bill get fired?

"I hear you," said Dr. Dupuis.

"You'll fuckin' hear me now. I'm taking Dr. Chia. I'm taking your stock. Lori and me are getting out safe. That's what I told her."

Safe. Ah. My brain finally clicked. He'd stolen everything from the OR for his sister so that she wouldn't overdose on some unlabelled street Fentanyl analogue. She'd run through the stash, and he'd gotten fired. Now he had nothing to lose. He'd clean us out or die trying.

"Bill," said Dr. Dupuis.

"You heard me. Amber gets the drugs, I get Dr. Chia. I'm taking her out. Give me the code if you like your knee caps."

I winced, my head still against the tile. *Taking her out* could also mean killing her.

"Amber, hurry the fuck up. I want Fentanyl, Morphine, Dilaudid, Percocet, Oxycodone, Tramadol. If it's a narcotic, I want it. Oh, and give me all your Ketamine. I'll take your Versed too. All the benzos. I want the vials. I want the pills. I want syringes and clean needles too."

Ripping off the OR. Bringing a bomb to the ER. Shooting at me. Wiping out our entire drug supply. Even the nurses' union couldn't fight those charges. Not right away, anyway.

"Don't you have any left over?" said Dr. Dupuis, confirming Bill as the OR thief.

"No! She needed them all! And after you numb nuts turned me in, I had to sell whatever I could."

"Bill. Your sister is a sick woman."

"Then why didn't you help her? Why did you let the police drag her away?"

"She attacked one of our staff."

Oh, shit. I tried to make myself as inconspicuous as possible while lying flat on the floor, in scrubs.

"Yeah? Why shouldn't she? Hell, I'll finish the job off myself. I won't miss the second time."

"Bill. You can't kill our people here." Dr. Dupuis sounded like he was explaining an algebra problem.

"Yeah? Watch me. As soon as I've got my stuff—hurry UP, Amber!" he called.

"I have to enter all different patients' names to unlock the machine! They won't let me take it out!" she shouted back, but her voice barely carried to my muffled ears.

"We're a family. Patrick was a part of us," said Dr. Dupuis.

"Who's Patrick," Bomb Guy's electro-voice replied.

I frowned at the floor. He didn't know the name of the guard he'd killed in vengeance?

Dr. Dupuis hesitated. "The security guard."

"Charles *Packard?* I'll get him on the way out. Hell, if he comes in, I'll blow him up. Serves him right. Smug bastard."

"No. The young one," said Dr. Dupuis, after a pause.

"He cuffed me too tight. I told Lori. Did she bite him or something?"

"No, not Lori," said Dr. Dupuis, after another pause.

True. The upside of a Code White and police escort was the perfect alibi. However, Dr. Dupuis took it in a different direction.

"Listen, I want to talk to you about your sister. I reviewed her chart. She was here a few weeks ago."

"Yeah. She needed a refill, and no one would give it to her. That's why I had to take the stuff from the OR."

I kept my eye roll to myself. Face down, no one would spot it.

Dr. Dupuis continued, "She had lab work with Dr. Callendar that found a slightly high potassium and low sodium."

My breath caught. I'd mentioned her electrolyte abnormalities before she tried to garrotte me with my own stethoscope.

"Yeah, he told her to follow up with her family doctor. It takes her five months to get in!" Bill's electronic voice beeped a few times, as if it couldn't process the next few words.

Dr. Dupuis continued, "That visit, she was vomiting and had abdominal pains. The triage nurse commented on her thin body habitus."

"I know. She was in withdrawal, all right? That's why I'm here!"

"She's in withdrawal," Dr. Dupuis agreed evenly, "but she may have a comorbid illness called Addison's disease, or adrenal insufficiency."

I gasped so loudly that it triggered a mini coughing fit.

Mind. Blown.

28

"What's that," said Bomb Guy.

"It's an autoimmune disease that attacks your adrenal glands," said Dr. Dupuis. "It means you can't produce cortiosol, even though your brain keeps telling it to make more."

In the midst of the world's worst night shift, Dr. Dupuis had reviewed the chart of a patient who'd already left the ER and made the diagnosis that the rest of us had missed.

While my coughs subsided, and Dr. Dupuis explained, I mentally reviewed her signs and symptoms: painfully thin. Abdominal pain. Nausea and vomiting. Eating salty chips, which made her pain complaints seem ludicrous, but helped her replenish her low sodium. Plus she was so darned tanned in January. I thought she was doing *bronzage*, but I vaguely remembered that excess ACTH stimulates melanin.

Bomb Guy didn't speak for a minute. "Why didn't anyone say that."

"It's very rare. Your sister didn't come here often—"

So rare that I'd never seen a case of Addison's. I only remembered it from an endocrinologist's lecture in first year medical school. He said that it struck 1 in 100,000 people.

"She came here, saw Callendar," said Bomb Guy.

"Right. He ordered blood work."

"Yeah, and nothing else. Useless twat."

That, Bill and I could agree on. Except it was insulting to female genitalia.

"And that bitch of a resident—" Bomb Guy went on.

Hey.

"An excellent addition to our department," Dr. Dupuis said, as if Bomb Guy had praised me. At least, I hoped God meant me and not Dr. Callendar.

"You all suck," said Bomb Guy.

So many compliments. My diagnostic brain had switched off when Lori had tried to throttle and stab me, but Addison's made so much sense. Except she'd seemed agitated. Shouldn't she be exhausted instead?

The woman was addicted to narcotics. Bill had raided the benzos and Ketamine too, either for her or for resale or a personal celebration. Benzos should bring her down. However, once you'd enjoyed the entire hospital pharmacopeia, as I'd realized earlier, Lori could have mixed in cocaine or PCP.

So if Lori Goody was mainlining everything up her nose and mouth and through her veins, that would boost her energy levels back to normal and beyond. And might explain the judgment: impaired.

"Where are my drugs. I want those and Dr. Chia, and if I don't get them in five minutes, I'm blowing you all to hell," Bomb Guy intoned.

"What kind of bomb is it?" said Dr. Dupuis.

"I'm not telling you jack shit. You'll probably come up with something two hours later, like you did with my sister."

"I know you're frustrated, but I can help Lori. You can, too."

I saw where Dr. Dupuis was going with this. *Don't blow us up, man. We're useful. You need us. And remember, if you take us down, you're taking yourself down, too.*

Since Bomb Guy hated me, it was better for me to do nothing and pray that he forgot "that bitch of a resident," much as it galled me. They also serve, those who lie on the floor.

"We're friends, right?" said Dr. Dupuis. "I haven't had a chance to talk to anyone else about the Addison's disease."

Don't blow me up, or your sister's diagnosis will get blown up, too.

"You told me. Now I know."

"Yeah, but I haven't assessed her myself yet. Let me take a look. You know I can help."

You know I'm God and I'll bring something new to the table. Don't blow us up.

"You all suck," Bill repeated, but softer now.

"You used to call us your family."

Bill made a spitting noise.

"We're a dysfunctional family for sure. I don't pretend we're great. But if you let us out of here, I promise that I'll do what I can to help you and Lori."

"You can't get me my job back. I'm finished."

Dr. Dupuis shook his head. "I can't promise that you'll get this job back—"

I sure as hell hope not, seeing as he's threatening to bomb us to death.

"—but I wouldn't rule anything out."

"Even if I could get a job in a nursing home somewhere, my pension is gone. My seniority is dead. No, you know I'll be in jail for the rest of my life. Lori will die without me."

Dr. Dupuis didn't blink. "You can work in other ways. You could be a motivational speaker. You could reach people on YouTube."

True. Bomb Guy could be born again on the Internet, preaching fire and explosions. Scary.

"There are other possibilities," said Dr. Dupuis. "You're worried about your sister's health. I can help with that. I can help you too."

Bill hesitated.

"We take care of everyone here, Bill. You know that and I know that. Sometimes, when you're in health care, you care a little too much. But I'll do what I can. And I can do a hell of a lot."

I could relax under God. All I had to do was call 911, and he'd take care of the rest, diagnosing and consoling would-be killers.

Something tapped to my right, around 4 o'clock, beyond the nursing station. Something that both silenced and inflamed the entire department.

I craned my neck and swivelled on the tile, straining to see. The counters blocked me. I had to thrust myself backwards, out of the nursing station, in order to understand.

From the shadow of the little hallway that led to the staff physician call room, Dr. Chia stared back at us.

29

D r. Chia could have gotten away. She could have snuck out of the building, unseen, through the door into the hallway. Instead, she'd entered the lair with the beast and the bomb.

Dr. Dupuis's face iced over.

She returned his gaze before she fixed on Bill, who studied her through the holes of his face mask. "Excellent. Come here, Dr. Chia. On my left side."

The side farther from Dr. Dupuis, who stood at 11 o'clock, on Bomb Guy's right, while Dr. Chia hovered at 4 o'clock.

"No." Dr. Dupuis tried to cut directly through the nursing station toward her.

"Don't move," Robo Bill commanded, raising his gun to Dr. Dupuis.

God ignored him as he exited the nursing station, circling the Plexiglass wall counterclockwise as he strode toward Dr. Chia. "She has nothing to do with this. Let her go."

"She has everything to do with this. We need funding. She has money."

"She doesn't." Dr. Dupuis had marched all the way to 6 o'clock without getting shot. Unfortunately, it meant that Bomb Guy now pointed the gun directly over me as he tracked him.

"Dave. Stop now, or I will blow your head off." His gloved fingers flexed around the trigger.

Dr. Dupuis halted, hands in the air, now less than 15 feet from Dr. Chia. She hadn't budged, apart from breathing.

"Don't shoot her. Never shoot her. She's innocent," said Dr. Dupuis.

Bill snorted. "No one is innocent. Don't you know that, Dave? You know what she is? *Useful.*"

Hmm. That didn't bode well for me, the "useless piece of shit."

Bill shifted his arms so that the gun now pointed at her head. He'd have to shoot her through the Plexiglass, but no one would bank on St. Joe's construction to protect us. "Tell your boyfriend to sign over 1.1 million dollars, or I'll blow you up."

Dr. Chia's eyes widened. She hadn't said a word. She looked fragile, and very beautiful, as she hovered in the shadows with her right hand raised to the doorway opening.

"You were trying to ransom me for 1.1 million dollars?" I muttered to the specks in the tile.

Bill didn't bother to shift his gaze or his gun, but he did deign to respond. "That was a mistake."

"I'll say." Couldn't he tell me and Dr. Chia apart in the parking lot? We didn't look much alike. They'd worked together for years, she was ten years older than me, and he still tried to kidnap me instead of her?

"Shut up." Now he pointed the pistol between my eyes.

I gulped. *Why* hadn't I shut up? Had fatigue eaten holes in my brain, like prions in Creutzfeldt-Jakob disease?

"I hired two shit-for-brains. They couldn't even grab the right chink. So fuck them. They're gone."

He must have killed them before he came in. They knew too much, and he clearly subscribed to the scorched earth strategy.

Which meant that I was next. He could use me as an object lesson for Dr. Chia, i.e., obey me, or this will happen to you.

Bomb Guy wouldn't miss a second time, in front of all these witnesses.

Ryan, Tucker, Kevin, Mom, Dad, Grandma, Other Grandma, Grandpa. I love you.

I squeezed my eyes shut, waiting for the bullet.

No. That reminded me of the famous Vietnam War picture of a poor man getting his brains blasted out.

I opened my eyes and glared at Bill as best I could from the floor, levering myself back into in cobra position. I'd die defiant.

Something slapped the tile floor. No, more of a shuffling noise, behind me and to my right. Say, five o'clock.

"Don't move," instructed Robo Bill.

I hadn't broken from cobra pose. He didn't mean me.

He meant whoever was walking, or dragging, toward us.

"Please, Alyssa..." Andrea whispered.

Alyssa. My sister in near-strangulation. Risen from Room 13.

Bill's head shifted toward her. I could feel his concentration break.

From the sound of it, Alyssa shambled toward us, slow but determined, like a zombie.

No one dared speak. They didn't want to draw Bomb Guy's attention. His gun stayed trained on me, and they wanted to keep it that way.

"Stop right there." Bomb Guy ordered, quieter than before. He enjoyed yelling at me and, to a certain extent, Dr. Dupuis, but he didn't know how to handle a small female whose blackened eyes, swollen face, bruised throat, and battered body advertised violence against women.

"You should lie down—" Roxanne started, but when Bill swung his gun in her general vicinity, she shut up, too.

"I don't want to hurt you," Bill told Roxanne. His gun pointed more at her feet than at her body. He still cared about his last friend.

"So don't do this." Roxanne looked at his face, at his eye holes, instead of the gun, as she took a step toward him. "You need help, Bill. We'll get it for you. You don't have to do this. You haven't hurt anyone yet—"

"You. Killed. Patrick," said Alyssa. Her footsteps stopped on my right. Out of my peripheral vision, I saw her sway on her feet. She'd fall on top of me.

I flinched. Dr. Dupuis on my left, Alyssa on my right, and me on the floor. All dead ducks, even if Alyssa didn't faint on me first.

Roxanne moved to catch her, but Bill redirected his gun, this time at Roxanne's chest. His arms trembled visibly.

There were too many of us. He couldn't shoot everyone at once with a .45. But if we got him panicked, he'd use the bomb.

"You killed Patrick because he walked you out." Alyssa's voice broke.

"No," said Robo Bill, raising his pistol at her. "Shut up, you stupid—"

Everything exploded then.

30

The ground shook beneath my body.

Warm liquid hit my neck.

Something banged into the back of my head—a body part? Shrapnel?

Not heavy enough for Alyssa, or for any adult body.

I'd covered my ears.

Still couldn't block out the screaming.

Hell, I was screaming too, with my shred of a voice.

But more than anything, I needed to know where that fucking Bomb Guy was.

Smoky air clogged my nose and fogged my eyes.

I strained to see as I boosted myself up to standing, stepping over fallen ceiling tiles.

Dr. Dupuis dragged Alyssa on her back by the ankles, toward the little hallway. Toward Dr. Chia, who rushed forward to help him.

Alyssa's mouth moved before she tried to knock Dr. Dupuis's hands away, so she was in fighting form.

Patients thrashed and sobbed in their thin, blue gowns, although my chest pain patient ripped off his monitor leads and took off for the exit across from him, near the light boxes.

I turned toward the smoking remnants of the nursing station.

A computer had toppled off a blackened, blasted counter, smashing its monitor. I stepped on an entire sheet of intact Plexiglass.

The secretary cowered under what was left of her desk, her lipsticked mouth shaping sounds I couldn't hear.

"My legs! My legs!" someone bellowed from three o'clock, but his yells meant he maintained his airway and breathing, and Dr. Dupuis had turned to check on him.

I'd make sure Bomb Guy was dead. Priority number one in first aid: secure the scene.

Or more bombs could detonate.

I scanned the wreckage. The smoke started to clear, although bright flames burned anew inside a recycling bin and its neighbouring trash can.

Bomb Guy lay ten feet away, at two o'clock, a twitching mound of blood and flesh.

Julie screamed and pointed at his head, which lay another ten feet beyond. His head had literally been blown off.

I have never thrown up during my medical training or while discovering dead bodies. I'm more of a fight than flight person.

This time, though, I had to twist my face to the left and fight the nausea. It took me a second of breathing through my teeth, while trying not to suck in the smoke or any aerosolized blood and body parts.

When I turned back, they were pushing a stretcher over the plaster and particle board and whatever else littered the floor.

Trying to get to Roxanne.

Roxanne lay on the ground, right hand clamped over her left arm, mid-humerus level. The rest had been blown away.

"I'm okay," she seemed to be saying as they boosted her up. Blood rained from her stump.

"Tourniquet," I said, sprinting to resus ahead of the stretcher.

I snatched a blue stretchy rubber band off one of the venipuncture carts right as they rolled in with Roxanne. I tied it firmly above her injury without stopping for gloves.

Roxanne's lips shaped the word "Thanks" as we attached her to the cardiac monitor.

Tears tracked down Andrea's cheeks as she pushed up Roxanne's pink scrub pants to get an IV in her foot. Which she did. First try. "Give me an Opsite."

Amber handed her one to secure that IV, while Linda inserted a second in her other leg.

Roxanne shook her head and joked, "You think they can do something with that?" She pointed at the charred forearm remnant, which someone had located and placed beside her stump.

What did I tell you? ER nurses. Tough breed.

Roxanne's BP clocked in at 122/78, heart rate 111, resp rate an even 18 with a sat of 99 percent. She would goddamn fucking pull through this.

While I called out orders for labs and X-rays—not that the nurses wouldn't have done all that anyway, on autopilot—I tried to puzzle out what had happened.

Bill's bomb had exploded, but how? He'd pointed his gun at Alyssa. Using both hands.

I wheeled around in a 360, surveying the area for more attackers.

Maybe one of Bill's parking lot minions had survived and sought revenge.

Maybe—please not this—Tucker had returned and fired on the most obvious threat.

Instead, my eyes focused on the lone figure lingering outside the resuscitation room.

Charles Packard, the head security guard, gripped a gun in both hands.

His eyes fixed on Bomb Guy's corpse.

I opened my mouth, but directly across from us, the light box doors flung open and shut again.

Blinding white light.

One more blast.

31

S moke.

More ceiling tiles raining down on us, exposing black pipes that reminded me of broken teeth.

Screams sounded thready now.

I dove to the floor, protecting what remained of my eardrums.

"POLICE! GET DOWN!"

I dared to to turn slightly toward the light box door. Even peering up through the clouds of smoke, my watery eyes detected a line of black figures. The first carried a black shield prominently emblazoned with a single word in white: POLICE.

"POLICE! GET DOWN!"

Police pointed gigantic assault rifles at us. They also sported helmets, gas masks and body armor, but I concentrated on the assault rifles.

I heard St. Joe's staff drop to the ground around me.

Charles Packard spun to face the officers. He adjusted his gun before he tossed it to the ground a metre to his right and knelt on the tile, hands straight up like telephone poles, and shouted, "The suspect has been neutralized."

The police fanned through the ambulance bay, each staking a position.

"POLICE! ON YOUR KNEES, HANDS UP!"

Uh oh. I was on my stomach, technically disobeying them.

I risked shifting onto my elbows, which raised me above the worm's eye view. My neck was getting tired anyway. Luckily, it wasn't hard to balance on those elbows, tuck my knees underneath me, and come up to kneel, raising my arms as straight as Charles Packard's.

An officer stalked perilously close to me, but he paused at Charles's gun before aiming his assault rifle at the man himself.

"The suspect has been neutralized!" Charles repeated.

I couldn't read the officer's expression under the gas mask, and my clogged ears couldn't process much of anything, but he must have called another officer, because a second, slightly shorter officer bagged the gun while the first officer kept his gun locked and loaded on the security guard.

"I know it's against the rules for a security officer to carry a firearm," said Charles Packard, keeping his hands up. "We're licensed for a taser and a baton, but no higher level weapons. Still, when Dr. Chia told me about the bomb, I notified you and came to assess the situation myself."

The hairs rose on the back of my neck. Somehow, Dr. Chia had woken up to the Code Black. She must have called 911 and snuck out her back door to inform the head of security.

And then she'd returned to the ER, risking her own life.

The taller officer said something I didn't catch, and Charles Packard let them handcuff his wrists behind his back. "I'm not denying anything. You have the firearm. You can run tests on it. I knew it was dangerous, but I'm an excellent shot. I took a calculated risk in taking out the suspect."

"Found two more!" shouted an officer, nudging two men out of the conference room hallway.

Two men I recognized.

Two men who must have unlocked the conference room door

with their skeleton key, only when Dr. Chia had hovered in the hallway and attracted Bomb Guy's attention, they had frozen behind her.

"Don't shoot! We're security guards!"

Michel and David thrust their hands in the air and dropped to their knees.

David's nose twitched. Michel drew back from the smoke, the charred fibreboard, and the cries inside the ER.

"Those are my men, the security guards of St. Joseph. I called them in for backup," said Charles.

I couldn't hear if the officers replied, but the shorter one didn't lower his weapon.

"I needed my firearm when I entered the emergency department," said Charles. "I knew it was against the rules. I knew I'll be fired and tried in a court of law, but I needed to rescue these people. I've worked here for thirty years. This is my family."

"What about Patrick?" I called. More coughing. I willed my vocal cords to function. "Patrick Warren, the security guard shot in the throat tonight."

"Yes, absolutely tragic," said Charles, never breaking eye contact with the taller officer.

I cut in. "Two indigenous visitors were beaten on New Year's, when Patrick Warren was on duty. So were you, Mr. Packard, along with David and Michel here."

"That very unfortunate case is under investigation right now, so I can't comment. You understand," Charles returned.

"*You* won't comment, but Patrick was going to. That's why he wore a suit the other day, right? To see his lawyer. To testify against you for using undue force."

Charles frowned. David watched his mentor for cues, but I could read the agony in Michel's hunched posture.

"You felt betrayed," I said to Charles. "You took Patrick in when he failed the police force exams. You were like a father to him."

Charles gave the slightest nod.

"But you're not the law." I turned to Michel and David. "Did you two shoot Patrick for him tonight?"

David's core muscles tensed under his blue shirt.

Michel licked his lips.

"Don't answer her," said Charles.

I kept my eyes on Michel. He was the one who was the most like Patrick, the one most broken by his death. They'd probably been friends.

Michel stared back at me, eyes glazed.

David shook his head. "We don't say nothing without a lawyer."

"You don't need a lawyer," said Charles. "We didn't do anything wrong."

I peered in the direction of Bill's body on the other end of the ER.

Charles snapped then. His face flushed, and I noticed his knuckles blanch behind his back. "I saved your life."

"Thank you for shooting the bomber. But when his minions grabbed me in the parking lot, you left your station at the ER doors. Those men could've killed me or Dr. Chia." Coincidence? Or had Charles, the *smug bastard,* secretly aided and abetted Bill? I continued, "Afterward, maybe Patrick ran outside to try and catch them. Or you sent him out to round again. Either way, you or David or Michel shot him in the throat while everyone was fussing over me in the ER."

Michel's mouth opened.

"Shut up, *tabernac,"* hissed David.

Michel shook his head, still speechless, while someone shuffled toward us from four o'clock. It had taken her this long to make it over, and she was flanked by a third officer, but she had arrived, body rigid with pain and fury.

David sneered.

Michel averted his eyes. His body seemed to hinge in itself, trying to squeeze away from her.

"You told me that you'd leave us alone if I got him to change his mind," Alyssa said. "I was thinking about it. I wouldn't even talk to Patrick the last time I saw him." Her voice broke as she envisioned it.

She shook her head, willing her tears away before she spoke again. "He's dead now. I don't give a shit what happens to me. I'm going to put you two away for fucking up my face, and your boss away for killing the love of my life. Just watch me."

32

Alyssa's words continued to haunt me while I saw Roxanne off.

Roxanne waved a cheery, one-handed goodbye as the paramedics transported her to University College Hospital. "Don't worry, Andrea. I always wanted to be the bionic woman."

The bomb squad evacuated the emergency department. That was chaos in itself, but we followed their orders and got every patient and staff member out. Three of them had already left in handcuffs.

The police reeled us all into the station for questioning. After I finished my statement, I roamed the hall, asking for Alyssa.

A French black female officer answered me. "She's gone with her sister. She said she'll call you, and something about plastic surgery."

"Thanks." I smiled a little, imagining Alyssa putting her face—and eventually, her life—back together.

I grabbed a yellow taxi (could not deal with a bus or wait for an Uber right now, price be damned) and sank into the back seat, not caring about the dust on the window frame. Better than blood.

The sun had risen, shining bravely while people brushed snow off their car windshields. Like it was an ordinary day.

I checked my messages. Still nothing from Tucker, but I called my parents back. "I'm fine. Don't worry."

"Why would we worry?" said my father cheerily.

It took me several seconds to respond. I didn't want to stress them out if they hadn't checked the news. "Uh. Just letting you know."

"We were going to call you anyway," he said. "We're coming to Montreal next weekend."

"We'll stay with you!" my mom chimed in.

"I, uh..." Oh, God. I hadn't actually broken the personal news yet. I swallowed. My throat twitched, but obeyed me enough to issue the syllables without coughing. "I'm moving next weekend."

"What? You need us to help you move?"

"You could. But I'll, uh, have a roommate."

"You're getting a roommate?" said my little brother, Kevin. "Who is it?"

"It's not settled yet, but it would be...John Tucker." I said his name very quickly, in case it might come out more girlish that way.

"John Tucker?" my mom repeated. "Who's that?" From her slightly marvelling tone, it was clear that she might as well have been thinking, What *is that?*

My cheeks burned. "I'm sorry. I didn't want to tell you this way." *Worst. Night. Shift. Ever.* "You'll like him. He's a good guy."

"He?" repeated my father.

"Yes," I said. "You remember, when I got off the airplane...and with the hostage taking..." I didn't want to explain any more than I had to.

"You mean that pale one?" said my father.

"Right, with the blond hair!" Mom put in.

"He's her boyfriend," said Kevin.

"I thought Ryan was her boyfriend," Dad said slowly.

"He is—he was," I corrected myself. I was crying again. "He's not talking to me right now."

"Because after the airplane, you started going out with Tucker?" said my mother.

"Sure." It was close enough, and easier to explain than the fact that I'd been juggling Ryan and Tucker simultaneously, or as they might say, jerking them around, since August. I blew my nose.

"But why? Ryan is perfect!" said Mom.

"He is." My heart ached.

"Then why..."

"It doesn't matter!" said Kevin. "She had to pick one. She picked the white guy. Now he can be her bodyguard, okay?"

I almost laughed between my tears. My nine-year-old brother was the fastest on the uptake, but he smashed my heart. And what a cliché, to pick the white guy. It wasn't even true. Deep in my soul, I still couldn't choose. "I don't want to worry you."

"Do you have a cold? You sound like you have a cold," said Dad.

"Daddy!" Mom chided.

"What?"

"She's crying!" said Kevin. "She misses Ryan. But there was no way she could have both of them forever. And Ryan's okay. I talked to him through Discord last week—"

"You talked to Ryan? Where is he?"

"I don't know," said Kevin, after a pause. I couldn't tell if he was lying over the phone.

"Where did he go?" said my mother.

"I have to go to the bathroom," said Kevin.

"KEVIN!"

But he was gone, and my parents couldn't help me. At long last, I hung up when they promised to coax Kevin out of the bathroom to call me back. After I got a few hours sleep, I'd drive to Ottawa myself and wring it out of my brother if I had to.

My phone buzzed twice, like an angry hornet. New text message.

I found him.

I stared at the screen.

Was Tucker serious? Was he kidding me? Where was Ryan? Could I talk to him?

He's ok.

What did that mean? It certainly wasn't great. Also, I don't really like OK as an abbreviation. It felt cut short, an ominous omen when it came to Ryan. I started tapping out my response, but a third text bubble from Tucker stopped me.

I promised to leave him alone now.

That meant...

I love you. I'm coming home.

I texted back, *I love you too.*

Then I barraged him with questions. *Where was he? How did you find him?* I started to call him, but the next text came through first.

He was in a monastery.

Whoa. I shouldn't have been surprised, since God was Ryan's first love, way before I charted in his life.

On the other hand, how many guys headed to a monastery in the 21st century? *How did you find him?*

Terry

I'd die of old age before we got through this. I called Tucker to get the straight scoop. "How did you convince Terry to tell you?"

"Roxy."

That was bizarre. "What? You took Ryan's dog—"

"Terry was walking Roxy. Ryan had left her with Terry while he was retreating with the monks. Terry walked her early, before going to work. I hung outside the apartment with some dog biscuits."

This didn't hang together for me. "You're a stranger. Why would Terry tell you?"

"I brought Ryan's mother too."

Truly strange. "You stopped by Mr. and Mrs. Wu's house in the middle of the night—"

"I reached out to her. She was frantic. Willing to try anything. I got her to calm down, and she told me to go to Terry's house. 'He knows something,' she said."

"Why didn't she do it herself?"

I could almost hear Tucker shrug. "She's not you, babe."

"And Mr. Wu let her go with you? My new boyfriend?"

"He came, too."

"Do I have to pry all of this out of you?"

He sort of laughed. "You want a play by play?"

"Of course. You should have videoed it."

He sighed. "Mrs. Wu was almost out of control. Well, you heard her. Not knowing where her son was—she needed to know that he was okay, right? Mr. Wu was finally willing to call the police, but she said it would be better to put the pressure on Terry. She had me sleep over at their house, and then bundled us out of there at 5:00 a.m. so we could wait for him to go to work. When we saw him with Roxy—"

"What was he doing with Roxy? She should have been with Rachel, the other dog foster person."

"She flaked out, I guess. That was why Ryan had Roxy in the first place, even though he knew he couldn't take her to the monastery. He had to bring Terry in at the last minute, and Terry was a bit burnt, having to look after a dog and work and come home at lunch to walk her and stuff. Once I offered to take Roxy off his hands—"

"You have *Roxy* now?" My new boyfriend was looking after my ex-boyfriend's dog?

"Mr. and Mrs. Wu aren't crazy about dogs, and Terry had some stuff at work that was taking him into overtime. I said I could do it. I like dogs, and my family will always help. No big."

My head spun. It hadn't worked out for the two of us to adopt another dog, and now Tucker had a hold of Ryan's dog. "He's going to kill you."

"Nah. He'll be all spiritual after meditating for two weeks, or whatever it is they do in monasteries."

"I wouldn't count on it. You'd better get Roxy back to his parents first."

"Yeah, they said they'd take her if they had to. They want Ryan more than anything. They'd put up with a fire-spitting monkey or a drunk polar bear."

There was stuff I didn't understand. Like why Ryan hadn't told his parents where he was going. That pushed against everything he'd stood for.

"They're driving down to the monastery this morning."

I rubbed my eyelids, beyond tired, but Ryan could drag me back from the gates of hell. I'd catch a few z's and head out. "Okay. Where?"

"Uh uh. Can't tell you, babe."

"What?" My voice was so loud that the taxi driver slammed on the brakes before staring at me reproachfully.

"That was part of the condition. You can't know. You can't go. He was super clear about that."

"Ryan was, or Terry?"

"Both, babe. You're...persona non grata."

I bet they called me worse than that. I squeezed my eyes shut and forced myself to count every blessing instead of keening.

No one had blown me up last night. My heart still thumped inside my chest. Ryan was alive, avoiding both suicide and homicide. He'd run back to God. He might vomit if he ever caught sight of me again, but he was alive on this earth and rebuilding his life. Without me.

My hand spasmed on my phone. I opened and closed my mouth soundlessly, reminding myself of Michel, the security guard.

The driver glanced at me in the rearview mirror.

I clapped my hands over my own face to cover my grief. In the end, only Ryan's parents would visit him. I wouldn't get to sob all over his manly chest. Tucker wouldn't get to gloat in real time that he'd gotten the girl.

Anyone who didn't have impaired judgment would say that was for the best.

"Okay," I finally managed to force out.

"Okay." Tucker deliberately lightened his tone. "I'm coming back to you. Was your night shift okay?"

I cracked up laughing. Clearly, he hadn't checked my messages, any of his favourite social media platforms, or the news. I'd so limited my texts to loving reassurance that I'd fooled him.

"No," I said, gazing at the silent, black apartment building standing before me. I refused to check the cemetery on the opposite side of the the street as I counted out the driver's fare plus a two dollar tip. "It wasn't okay."

"Aww. Were you up all night?"

"Yeah. You could definitely say that." I zipped my wallet in my backpack and heaved it across both shoulders.

His tone shifted. "Hope. You didn't...meet any murderers, did you?"

I slammed the door behind me and laughed so hard that it made me cough.

I waved as the taxi sped away, still coughing and now enveloped in car exhaust. My kingdom for some warm water, honey, and lemon. I should have at least swiped another butterscotch candy on my way out of the ER.

Tucker swore. "I'm coming."

Why didn't he know this already? I checked my text to him about bullets in the parking lot. Autocorrect had changed it to *bullies* in the parking lot.

"I'm on my way. Are you okay?" he asked.

I cackled again. I might have fooled someone less observant, but Tucker's voice tightened. "Oh, God, Hope. Not again. I'm pulling over, you can tell me everything—"

"Don't get into an accident," I said, sobering up. I'd rather deliberately keep him in the dark, the way we sometimes did when calling in families for a Code Blue, saying that their loved one was "very sick," rather than give them news over the phone and risk a car crash. "I'm fine. FINE, as Louise Penny would say."

"Fucked-up, Insecure, Neurotic, and Egotistical?" he said. He'd read her books, too.

"Exactly. And breathing. So take it slow and easy. I'm...no more screwed up than usual, okay?"

"Okay," he said, but for the first time, Roxy barked, sensing his mood.

"Hello, Roxy. Well, I've got to go," I said. My voice cracked. I needed to rest every part of me. The cold January air stung my nose.

"You've got to chart?" he said. "Your shift's over."

"No, for once, I think they don't care too much about charting," I said, remembering the smashed computer at the nursing station. I laughed again. "SARKET is at a standstill for now."

My ears rang. I felt grit under my eyelids and microscopic blood cemented to my skin and clothes. I had to shower before I crashed.

Even so, I gave Tucker a loud smack through the phone, and he pretended to kiss me right back.

AFTERWORD

I checked a research paper online during my emergency day shift. A headline popped up, something about an accused neurosurgeon, but I didn't have a chance to process anything until after that shift on December 4th, 2016.

Then I realized that Dr. Elana Fric had been killed.

So many of my physician friends grieved openly. They knew and loved her as a gifted family physician, the devoted mother of three children, a leader in the Ontario Medical Association. They raised money for her parents and children. They wrote to the press and shifted headlines and news stories to focus on her achievements instead of her husband's. They appeared in court during her former husband's trial, where he eventually pled guilty to and was convicted of second degree murder.

My colleagues posted articles on intimate partner violence (IPV), the newer term for domestic violence which includes current and former relationships. I was most shocked by "Non-fatal strangulation is an important risk factor for homicide of women" (https://www.ncbi. nlm.nih.gov/pmc/articles/PMC2573025/).

Bottom line: if he almost chokes you to death, and you manage to survive, he will probably kill you later.

If you're African-American, it's not as strong a risk factor—you're "only" 4.65 times as likely to die—because your risk of getting killed in general is *already* four times higher than a white or Latina woman. And because your partner is more likely to abuse you by near-strangling, even if he or she doesn't kill you.

I cried when I read that.

I cried for Elana, whom I had never met and now would never meet. I cried for the African-American women, and the Latina women, and the white women in that study. I cried because even without reading a Canadian study, I knew that indigenous women would be abused at a higher rate (and I was right. Here's the proof. Reports of near-strangling decreased for the other Canadian groups, but went *up* for indigenous women: https://www.ncbi.nlm.nih.gov/pmc/articles/PMC4202982/). I cried for the Asian and African women who weren't surveyed in either study.

Then I tried to figure out what I could do.

In the emergency room, I now ask all patients with an injury, "Is someone hurting you?" That applies to any gender, any age, with any signs of injury, since the Center for Disease Control estimates that IPV affects 1 in 5 women and 1 in 12 men. For a child, I ask the caregiver.

I get a lot of strange looks. More than one woman held up her fist and replied, "No. If anyone tried to hurt me, I'd give it to him." One said yes, but wasn't ready to leave yet. We talked about safer ways to do this.

When IPV strikes friends of friends, as it crosses all ethnicities and walks of life, I have offered our home as a safe haven. We may have a loud Rottweiler, too many deer flies and too much clutter, but it is safe.

When the Canadian Women in Medicine asked for silent auction donations for the Fric family, I wondered if I should donate my Unfeeling Doctor non-fiction books.

"You should donate your Hope Sze series!" said the organizer, Dr. Jennifer Upitis.

Well. I didn't want to seem insensitive, treating crime as entertainment, but she told me they wouldn't see it that way. I should go for it.

At the cocktail party itself, I felt too embarrassed to venture near the silent auction table, in case Hope and I didn't raise any money, but a nephrologist at the snack table said, "Looks like your books are the high bid item tonight."

My books? Really?

I hurried over as the auction closed. Dr. Amie Padilla had made the winning bid: $400. "It's a good cause," she said, and changed it to $500.

Hang on. I got something in my eyes for a second there.

When I recovered, I decided that if crime novels could raise money for a good cause, then I would dedicate *Graveyard Shift* to Elana and donate some of the proceeds to help her family, as well as some to help people in my own area, especially indigenous women.

As a reader, you're helping to complete the circle. *Niawen'kó:wa,* which means thank you very much in Kanienkehaka (Mohawk).

ACKNOWLEDGMENTS

S, thank you for the story that inspired *Graveyard Shift*. Thank you for the hours you and your brothers and sisters serve, day and night, to make our world a safer place.

Canadian women in medicine, you make the world a better place, whether it's in the hospitals or at home or online. You work so hard, and yet you retain your sense of humour and generosity. Kudos to you and all physicians keeping our health care system afloat and sometimes even thriving.

Big ups to the nurses, the orderlies, the security guards, secretaries, and the rest of our team who toil day and night. I rely heavily on you, most especially during night shifts. I gave you more complicated roles in *Graveyard Shift*, which meant going to some dark places. As Ursula K. Le Guin wrote in *A Wizard of Earlhsea,* "To light a candle is to cast a shadow..."

Nicole Spahich not only answered all my questions, but prepared notes and took me out to lunch at Family Circle Restaurant! It doesn't get any better than that. Next one's on me.

Permanent thanks to Ed Adach, forensic detective at the Toronto Police Service, who does his best to respond to my e-mails, even while in the Netherlands, taking a course on clandestine graves.

The Writers Police Academy introduced me to good people who give me good advice, including Paul M. Smith, Colleen Belongea, and Mike Knetzger.

Shihan Tom Bellazzi, 7th Dan, and Sensei Dan Desjardins, 3rd Dan, at the Ken Sei Kai Academy of Martial Arts, weighed in on my fight scenes.

RN Margaret MacDonald sought out my editorial gremlins.

SF Canada is a treasure trove of kind brains.

Maggie Lynch, at Windtree Press, always goes above and beyond, even as she builds her own writing career.

Graveyard Shift took me on a complicated journey, as I wrote it partly during National Novel Writing Month and between trips to Ecuador and Egypt. It was originally twice the length before ruthless cutting, so I truly appreciated my husband, Matt, saying, "It's good. I look forward to reading a version that's more than 89 pages."

All errors are my own. Can't be a doctor or a writer without taking full responsibility.

Thanks for reading. If you enjoyed *Graveyard Shift*, please let your friends know and post a review. Join the Kamika-Sze mailing list at www.melissayuaninnes.com for a free book. And stay tuned for Hope #8, which is set in Egypt!

ABOUT THE AUTHOR

Melissa Yi is the pseudonym for an emergency physician and a proud finalist for the Arthur Ellis Award (best crime story in Canada) and the Derringer Award (best mystery story in the English language).

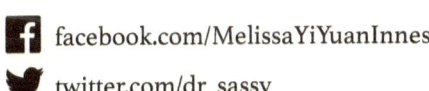 facebook.com/MelissaYiYuanInnes

twitter.com/dr_sassy

ALSO BY MELISSA YI

Code Blues (Hope Sze 1)

Notorious D.O.C. (Hope Sze 2)

Family Medicine (essay & Hope Sze novella combining the short stories *Cain and Abel, Trouble and Strife, and Butcher's Hook*, which are also available separately)

Terminally Ill (Hope Sze 3)

Student Body (Hope Sze novella post-Terminally Ill; includes radio drama *No Air*)

The Sin Eaters (Hope Sze short story and Arthur Ellis Award finalist)

Blood Diamonds (Hope Sze short story)

Stockholm Syndrome (Hope Sze 4)

Human Remains (Hope Sze 5)

Blue Christmas (Hope Sze short story)

Death Flight (Hope Sze 6)

Graveyard Shift (Hope Sze 7)

More mystery & romance novels by Melissa Yi

The Italian School for Assassins *(Octavia & Dario Killer School Mystery 1)*

The Goa Yoga School of Slayers *(Octavia & Dario Killer School Mystery 2)*

Wolf Ice

High School Hit List

The List

Dancing Through the Chaos

Mr. Chef & Ms. Librarian

www.ingramcontent.com/pod-product-compliance
Lightning Source LLC
Chambersburg PA
CBHW051254250626
47155CB00009B/3291